"I had heard you were between mistresses at present. I had so hoped to be the next."

His dark eyes flared, then turned to molten gold. She held his gaze as if she were as bold, as daring, as her words suggested. Hoping that she could be. She had to be.

"But of course," she continued, because this was the crux of it—because she knew Peter was listening and that she had to push the words out, no matter how they seemed to clog her throat, "as your mistress, I would require your generosity. A great deal of it."

For another endless moment Nikos only watched her, his gaze still searing through her—reducing her to ash, making her breath desert her—but otherwise his big body remained still, alert. It was almost as if she had not propositioned him. As if she had not offered to prostitute herself to him as casually as she might have ordered a drink from the bartender.

But then, making every hair on her body prickle, Nikos smiled.

It had been a long time in coming, this moment, and Nikos could not help but savor it. Revel in it. He had never dared dream that his archenemy's sister would offer herself to him as his mistress, thus ensuring his ultimate victory—his final revenge. But he would take it—and her.

All about the author...
Caitlin Crews

CAITLIN CREWS discovered her first romance novel at the age of twelve in a bargain bin at the local five-and-dime. It involved swashbuckling pirates, grand adventures, a heroine with rustling skirts and a mind of her own, and a seriously mouthwatering and masterful hero. The book (the title of which remains lost in the mists of time) made a serious impression. Caitlin was immediately smitten with romances and romance heroes, to the detriment of her middle school social life. And so began her lifelong love affair with romance novels, many of which she insists on keeping near her at all times, thus creating a fire hazard of love wherever she lives.

Caitlin has made her home in places as far-flung as York, England and Atlanta, Georgia. She was raised near New York City, and fell in love with London on her first visit when she was a teenager. She has backpacked in Zimbabwe, been on safari in Botswana, and visited tiny villages in Namibia. She has, while visiting the place in question, declared her intention to live in Prague, Dublin, Paris, Athens, Nice, the Greek Islands, Rome, Venice and/or any of the Hawaiian islands. Writing about exotic places seems like the next best thing to moving there.

She currently lives in California with her animator/comic-book-artist husband and their menagerie of ridiculous animals.

Caitlin Crews

KATRAKIS'S SWEET PRIZE

TORONTO • NEW YORK • LONDON
AMSTERDAM • PARIS • SYDNEY • HAMBURG
STOCKHOLM • ATHENS • TOKYO • MILAN • MADRID
PRAGUE • WARSAW • BUDAPEST • AUCKLAND

Recycling programs
for this product may
not exist in your area.

ISBN-13: 978-0-373-12980-5

KATRAKIS'S SWEET PRIZE

Previously published in the U.K. as KATRAKIS'S LAST MISTRESS

First North American Publication 2011

Copyright © 2010 by Caitlin Crews

This edition published by arrangement with Harlequin Books S.A.

For questions and comments about the quality of this book
please contact us at Customer_eCare@Harlequin.ca.

® and ™ are trademarks of the publisher. Trademarks indicated with
® are registered in the United States Patent and Trademark Office, the
Canadian Trade Marks Office and in other countries.

www.eHarlequin.com

Printed in U.S.A.

KATRAKIS'S SWEET PRIZE

To Liza, who dreamed of gold-eyed dragons,
Jane, who knew I couldn't pull that punch,
and Jeff, who makes it easy to write about heroes.

CHAPTER ONE

NIKOS KATRAKIS was by far the most dangerous man aboard the sleek luxury yacht. Ordinarily Tristanne Barbery would take one look at a man like him—so dark and powerful her breath caught each time she gazed at him from her place within sight of the elegant marble-topped bar where he stood—and flee for her life in the opposite direction.

Any man who seemed to dim the sparkling blue-green waters of the Mediterranean Sea with his very presence was far too complicated, far too *much* for Tristanne. *This is not about you,* she told herself fiercely, then ordered herself to release the fingers she'd clenched into fists. She willed away her nausea, her shakiness. Her panic. Because this was not, indeed, about Tristanne. It was about her mother and her mother's crippling, impossible debts. And she would do whatever she had to do to save her mother.

There were other rich and powerful men aboard the boat, rubbing expensively clad shoulders together while gazing at the glittering shores of the Côte d'Azure: the olive-clad hills and pastel waterfront facades of Villefranche-sur-Mer to the left, the red-topped villas of Cap Ferrat to the right, and the sparkling sweep of Villefranche Bay spread out around them in the late afternoon sun.

But Nikos Katrakis was different from the rest. It wasn't simply because he owned this particular yacht, though his ownership was as clear as a brand—almost visible, Tristanne thought; almost seeming to emanate from him in waves. It wasn't even the undeniable physical power he seemed to *just* restrain beneath his deceptively calm surface, even dressed as casually as he was, in denim trousers and a white dress shirt left open at the neck to display a swathe of dark olive skin.

It was *him*.

It was the way he stood, commanding and yet so remote, so alone, even in the center of his own party. There was a fierce, unmistakably male energy that hummed from him, attracting notice but keeping all but the most brave away. He would have been devastating enough if he were unattractive—he was that powerful.

But of course, Nikos Katrakis was not, in any sense of the word, unattractive. Tristanne felt a shiver of awareness trace its way down her spine, and she could not bring herself to look away. He was more powerful than her late father had been but not, she thought, as cold. And somehow she could sense that he was no brute, like her brother, Peter—a man so cruel he had refused to pay her mother's medical bills, a man so heartless he had laughed in the face of Tristanne's desperation.

Yet something about Nikos made her think he was different, made her think of dragons—as if he was that magical and that dangerous; as if he was epic. He was too virile. Too masculine. His power seemed to hum around him like an electric current. *Dragon*, she thought again, and her palms suddenly itched to sketch the bold, almost harsh lines of his face—though she knew that was exactly the sort of thing Peter so scorned. There was no explaining creativity to her overbearing brother.

But all of that was precisely why Nikos Katrakis was the only man who would do. She was wasting time simply gazing at him, trying to get up her nerve, when she knew Peter would be searching for her before too long. She knew he did not trust her, no matter that she had agreed to go along with his plan. And she would go along with it, or seem to, but she would do it on her terms, not his. And she would do so with the one man Peter hated above all others—the one man Peter viewed as his chief business rival.

She had moved beyond nervous into something else— something that made her pulse flutter and her knees feel like syrup. She could only hope that it didn't show, that he would see what her brother, Peter, claimed everyone saw when they looked at her: nothing but Barbery ice.

It's about time you used your assets to our advantage, Peter had said in his cold voice. Tristanne shook the memory away, determined not to react to him any further—even in her own mind. Not when so much was at stake. Her mother's survival. The independence she had fought so hard to win. Tristanne sucked in a fortifying breath, sent up a little prayer and forced herself to walk right up to Nikos Katrakis himself before she talked herself out of it.

Nikos looked up from his drink at the polished wood and marble-topped bar and their eyes met. Held. His eyes were the color of long-steeped tea, shades lighter than the thick, dark hair on his head and the dark brows that arched above, making them seem to glow like old gold. They seared into her. Tristanne's breath caught, and a restless heat washed over her, scalding her. The sounds of the high-class partygoers, their clinking glasses and cultured laughter, disappeared. Her anxiety and her purpose fell away as if they had never been. It was as if the whole world—the glittering expanse of the French Riviera, the endless blue-green Mediterranean Sea—faded into his hot, gold gaze. Was consumed by him, enveloped into him—*changed by him*, that fanciful voice whispered in the back of her mind.

"Miss Barbery," he said in greeting, his native Greek coloring his words just slightly, adding a rough caress to his voice. It sounded like a command, though he did not alter his careless position, lounging so indolently against the bar, one hand toying with his glass of amber-colored liquor. He watched her with old, intent eyes. The hairs on the back of Tristanne's neck stood at attention, letting her know that he was not at all what he seemed.

Something wild and unexpected uncoiled inside of her, making her breath stutter. Shocking her with its sudden intensity.

He was not careless. He was in no way relaxed. He was only pretending to be either of those things.

But then, she was banking on that. Surely her brother, who cared only about money and power, would not be as obsessed as he was about this man unless he was a worthy opponent.

"You know my name?" she asked. She managed to keep her composure despite the humming reaction that shimmered through her, surprising and unsettling her. It was the Barbery family trait, she thought with no little despair: she could appear to be perfectly unruffled while inside, she was a quivering mess. She had learned it at her father's emotionless knee—or suffered the consequences. And she wanted only to use this man for her own ends, not succumb to his legendary charisma. She had to be strong!

"Of course." One dark brow rose higher, while his full, firm lips twisted slightly. "I pride myself on knowing the names of all my guests. I am a Greek. Hospitality is not simply a word to me."

There was a rebuke in there somewhere. Tristanne's stomach twisted in response, while he looked at her with eyes that saw too much. Like he was a cat and she a rather dim and doomed mouse.

"I have a favor to ask you," she blurted out, unable to play the game as she ought to—as she'd planned so feverishly once she'd realized where Peter was taking her this afternoon. There was something in the way Nikos regarded her—so calm, so direct, so powerfully amused—that made her feel as if the glass of wine she'd barely tasted earlier had gone straight to her head.

"I'm so sorry," she murmured, surprised to feel a flush heating her cheeks. She, who up until this moment had considered herself unable to blush! "I wanted to work up to that. You must think I am the rudest person alive."

His dark brows rose, and his wicked mouth curved slightly, though his enigmatic eyes did not waver, nor warm. "You have not yet asked this favor. Perhaps I will reserve judgment until you do."

Tristanne had the sudden sense that she was more at risk, somehow, standing in front of Nikos Katrakis in full view of so many strangers than she was from Peter and his schemes. It was an absurd thought. *You must be strong!* she reminded herself, but she couldn't seem to shake that feeling of danger.

Or stop what came next. What had to come next—even though she knew, suddenly, with a deep, feminine wisdom that seemed like a weight in her bones, that this was a mistake of unfathomable proportions. That she was going to regret stirring up this particular hornet's nest. That she, who prided herself on being so capable, so independent, did not have what it took to handle a man like this. One should never rush heedlessly into a dragon's lair. Anyone who had ever read a fairy tale knew better! She bit her lower lip, frowning slightly as she looked at him, feeling as if she fell more and more beneath his dark gold spell by the moment. It was if he was a trap, and she had walked right into it.

The trouble was, that didn't seem to frighten her the way it should. And in any case, she had no choice.

"The favor?" he prompted her, something sardonic moving across his face. Almost as if he knew what she planned to ask him—but that was silly. Of course he could not know. Of all the things that Tristanne knew about Nikos Katrakis—that he was ruthless and magnetic in equal measure, that he had clawed his way from illegitimacy and poverty into near-unimaginable wealth and influence with the sheer force of his will, that he suffered no fools and tolerated no disloyalty, that he alone drove her cold brother into fits of rage with his every success—she had never heard it mentioned that he was psychic. He could have no idea what she wanted from him.

"Yes," Tristanne said, her tone even. Confident. In direct contrast to the mess of unsettled churning within. "A favor. But just a small favor, and not, I hope, an entirely unpleasant one."

She almost called it off then. She almost heeded the panicked messages her body and her intuition were sending her—she almost convinced herself that someone else would do, that she need not pick *this* man, that someone less intimidating would work just as well, could accomplish what she needed.

But she glanced to the side then, to ease the intensity of Nikos Katrakis's gaze and to catch her breath, and saw her brother shoulder his way into the bar area. *Half brother*, she reminded herself, as if that should make some difference. Peter's familiar scowl was firmly in place when he looked at her—and who she was with. Behind him, she saw the clammy-palmed financier Peter had handpicked for her—the man he had decreed would be his ticket out of financial ruin for the modest price of Tristanne's favors.

"You must bolster the family fortune," he had told her matter-of-factly six weeks earlier, as if he was not discussing her future. Her life.

"I don't understand," she had said stiffly, still wearing her black dress from their father's memorial service earlier that day. She had not been in mourning, not even so soon after his death. Not for Gustave Barbery, at any rate—though she would perhaps always grieve for the father Gustave had never been to her. "All I want is access to my trust fund a few years early."

That bloody trust fund. She'd hated that it existed, hated that her father thought it gave him the right to attempt to control her as he saw fit. Hated more that Peter was its executor now that her father was dead—and that, for her mother's sake, she had to play along with him in order to access it. She'd wanted nothing to do with the cursed Barbery fortune nor its attendant obligations and expectations. She'd spent years living proudly off of her own money, the money she'd earned with her own hands—but such pride was no longer a luxury she could afford. Her mother's health had deteriorated rapidly once Gustave fell ill; her debts had mounted at a dizzying rate, especially once Peter had taken control of the Barbery finances eight months ago and had stopped paying Vivienne's bills. It fell to Tristanne to sort it out, which was impossible on the money she made scraping out the life of an artist in Vancouver. She had no choice but to placate Peter in the hope she could use her trust to save her mother from ruin. It made her want to cry but she did not—*could not*—show that kind of weakness in front of Peter.

"You don't have to understand," Peter had hissed at her, triumph and malice alive in his cold gaze. "You need only do as I say. Find an appropriately wealthy man, and bend him to your will. How hard can that be, even for you?"

"I fail to see how that would help you," Tristanne had said. So formal, so polite, as if the conversation were either. As if she did not feel like giving in to her upset stomach, her horror.

"You need not concern yourself with anything save your own contribution," Peter had snapped. "A liaison with a certain caliber of man will make my investors more confident. And believe me, Tristanne, you'll want to ensure their confidence. If this deal does not go through, I will lose everything and the first casualty will be your useless mother."

Tristanne understood all too well. Peter had never made any secret of his disdain for Tristanne's mother. Gustave had put his empire in Peter's hands at the onset of his long illness, having cut off Tristanne for her rebelliousness years before. He had no doubt expected his son to provide for his second wife, and had therefore made no specific provision for her in his will. But Tristanne was well aware that Peter had waited years to make Vivienne Barbery pay for usurping his own late mother's place in what passed for Gustave's affections. He had dismissed her failing, fragile health as *attention-seeking*, and allowed her debts to mount. He was capable of anything.

"What do you want me to do?" Tristanne had asked woodenly. She could do it, whatever it was. She would.

"Sleep with them, marry them, I do not care." Peter had sneered. "Make certain it is public—splashed across every tabloid in Europe. You must do whatever it takes to convince the world that this family has access to serious money, Tristanne, do you understand me?"

On the Katrakis yacht, Tristanne looked away from the financier and back to Peter, whose gaze burned with loathing. And as easily as that, her indecision vanished. Better to burn out on Nikos Katrakis's fire—and annoy Peter in the process by *contributing* using his avowed worst enemy—than suffer a far more clammy and repulsive fate. Tristanne repressed a shudder.

When she returned her attention to Nikos Katrakis, the dragon, his half smile had disappeared. Though he still lounged against the bar, Tristanne sensed that his long, hard-muscled body was on red-alert. She had the sense of his physical might, of tremendous power hidden in casual clothes. It made her throat go dry.

This is a terrible mistake, she thought. She knew it in her bones. She felt it like an ache, a sob. But there was nothing to do but go for it.

"I would like you to kiss me," she said, very distinctly. And then there was no going back. It was done. She cleared her throat. "Here and now. If it is not too much trouble."

Of all the things Nikos Katrakis had expected might happen during the course of the afternoon's party, being solicited in any form by the Barbery heiress had not made the list.

A hard kind of triumph poured through him. He was sure that she could see it—sense it. How could she not?

But she only gazed at him, her eyes the color of the finest Swiss chocolate. A dark satisfaction threatened to get the best of him. He found himself smiling, not pleasantly—and still, she did not look away.

She was a brave little thing. Braver by far than her cowardly, dishonorable relatives.

Not that her bravery would help her much. Not with him.

"Why should I kiss you?" he asked softly, enjoying the flush that heated her skin, making her skin glow red and gold in the late afternoon light. He toyed with his glass, and indicated the throng around them with a careless flick of his wrist. "There are any number of women on this boat who would fight to kiss me. Why should it be you?"

Surprise shone briefly in her gaze, then was replaced by something else. She swallowed, and then, very deliberately, smiled. It was a razor-sharp society smile. Nikos did not mistake it for anything but the weapon it was.

"Surely there are points for asking directly," she said, her distractingly strong chin tilting up, her accent an unidentifiable yet attractive mix of Europe and North America. Her dark lashes swept down, then rose again to reveal her frank gaze. "Rather than lounging about in inappropriate clothing, hoping my décolletage might do the asking for me."

Nikos found himself very nearly amused, despite himself. Despite his urge to crush her—because she was a Barbery and

thus tainted, because he had vowed long ago that he would
not rest until they were all so much dust beneath his feet,
because her spineless worm of a brother watched them, even
now. He shifted closer to her, moving his body far nearer to
hers than was polite. She held her ground.

He wished he did not like it, but he did. Oh, how he did.

"Some women have no qualms about displaying whatever assets they possess to their best advantage," he said. He
placed his drink on the bar. "But I take your point."

He let his gaze travel over her—not for the first time,
though she could not know it. But today he had the pleasure
of letting her stand there and watch him as he did it. From
the gentle waves of her dark blonde hair, to her disarmingly
intelligent brown eyes, to the lithe figure she'd poured into
a simple shift dress that appreciated her curves almost as
much as he did, she was compelling—but more for the ways
in which she was not quite beautiful than for the ways she
was. The strong chin. The obvious intellect she did nothing
to conceal. The faint evidence that she did not spend her free
time injecting herself with Botox or collagen or silicone.
The signs of tension in her neck and shoulders that she was
trying to hide, that hinted at her reasons for such a request.
He dragged his attention back to her face, pleased to see a
hint of temper crack across her expression before she carefully hid it behind her polished social veneer.

"What can you bring to a kiss that another cannot?" he
asked, as if he was unimpressed with what he'd seen.

She did not retreat, or turn bright red with shame, as others
might have. She merely crooked one delicate eyebrow, challenging him. Daring him.

"Me," she said. Her expression added, *of course.*

Nikos felt desire flash through him, surprising him.
Shocking him. He had not expected it—he should, by rights,
despise her by association. But Tristanne Barbery was not at
all what he had imagined she would be. He had expected her

to be attractive. How could she not be? She had been schooled in the finest finishing schools in Europe, polished to the nth degree. He had looked at her in photographs over the years, and had found her to be natural, unstudied, though it was impossible to tell if that was a trick of the lens. He knew now that photographs could not do this woman justice. She was too alive—too vibrant—as if life danced in her, like a fire.

He wanted to touch it. Her.

And then he wanted to ruin her, just as Althea had been ruined and his father destroyed. Just as he, too, had been ruined, however temporarily. *Never again*, he vowed. Not for the first time.

"You make another good point," he agreed, his voice low as he fought off the dark memories. He reached across the space between them and pulled a long strand of her hair between his fingers. It felt like raw silk, soft and supple, and warm. Her lips parted slightly, as if she could feel his touch. He felt himself harden in response. "But I am not in the habit of kissing strange women in view of so many," he continued, his voice pitched for her ears alone. "It has a nasty habit of ending up in the tabloids, I find."

"I apologize," Tristanne murmured. Her clever eyes met his, daring him. "I was under the impression that you were renowned for your fearlessness. Your ability to scoff in the face of convention. Perhaps I have confused you for another Nikos Katrakis."

"I am devastated," he replied smoothly, his eyes on hers. He moved closer, and something inside him beat like a drum when she still did not step away. "I assumed it was my good looks that drew you to me, begging to be kissed. Instead you are like all the rest. Are you a rich man's groupie, Miss Barbery? Do you travel the world and collect kisses like a young girl collects autographs?"

"Not at all, Mr. Katrakis," she replied at once. She tilted her head back, and raised her brows in that challenging way of hers. "I find rich men are my groupies. They follow me around, making demands. I thought to save you the trouble."

"You are too kind, Miss Barbery." This time he traced the ridge of her collarbone, her taut, soft skin. He felt her tremble, just slightly, beneath his fingers, and almost smiled. "But perhaps I do not share what is mine."

"Says the man on a yacht filled with more guests than he can count."

"I have not kissed the yacht, nor the guests." He inclined his head. "Not all of them, that is."

"You must share your rules with me, then," she replied, her lips twitching slightly as if she bit back laughter. He did not know why he found that mesmerizing. "Though I must confess to you that I am surprised there are so many. So much for the grand stories of Nikos Katrakis, who bows to no tradition, follows no rule and forges his own way in this world. I think I'd like to meet *him*."

"There is only one Nikos Katrakis, Miss Barbery." He was so close now that her perfume filled the space between them, something subtle, with spice and only the faintest hint of flowers. He wondered if she would taste as sweet, with as much kick. "I hope it will not destroy you to learn that it is me."

"I have no way to judge what it will or will not do," she said, her eyes bold on his, "as you have not yet kissed me."

"Ah," he said. "And now it is an inevitability, is it?"

"Of course." She cocked her head to one side, and smiled. It was even more of a challenge, and Nikos had not become the man he was today by backing down from a challenge. "Isn't it?"

This was not what he had planned. Spontaneity was for those with less to lose, and far less to prove. He owed the late Gustave Barbery and his odious son, Peter, payback on the grandest scale, and he had spent the last decade making certain the opportunity would present itself, which it had, again and again. A push here, a whisper there, and the Barbery fortunes had taken a tumble, especially since the old man's illness—but he had not intended to involve the girl. He was not like the Barberys. He was not like Peter Barbery, who had seduced, impregnated and abandoned Althea with so much cold calculation. He refused to be like the Barberys! But then, he could not have predicted that his arch-enemy's sister would approach him in this way.

Or—more intriguing and far more dangerous—that she would tempt him to throw away the iron control he had worked so hard to maintain. He was not averse to using her or any other tool he could find that might lead to her family's destruction. But he could not have anticipated that he might want her—desire her—in spite of it all.

"I believe you may be right," he said quietly. Her bold expression faltered, just for the barest of moments, but Nikos saw it. And something in him roared in triumph. She was not as unaffected as she pretended to be. He did not care to explore why that should please him.

He reached over and slid his palm around to cup her nape. The contact sent electricity surging through him, desire and a deep hunger following like an echo. Her eyes widened, and her hands came up to rest on the hard planes of his chest.

He let the moment draw out, aware of the interested eyes on them from all corners of the yacht's entertainment deck, knowing that no matter what game she thought she was playing, she had no idea who she was dealing with. She had no idea what she'd set in motion by approaching him.

But he knew. He had already won this long, cold battle. She was simply the final straw that would destroy the Barbery empire once and for all, just as they had nearly destroyed him once upon a time.

He had finally done it—and yet instead of reveling in his

hard-won victory, his attention focused solely on the rich, lush curve of her lips.

He pulled her to him and fit his mouth to hers.

CHAPTER TWO

FIRE!

Tristanne would have screamed the word if she could.

Instead she kissed him. If that was the word for the slick, hot meeting of their mouths. If that was why every alarm in her body rang out *danger*, her stomach in knots and her skin ablaze with sensation, as if it was too small or she had grown too big to wear it any longer.

She had not thought too far beyond the simple request—she had not imagined what it would be like to kiss this man. Or, more precisely, to be kissed by him. He was elemental, untamed. He took. He demanded. He possessed.

And she could not seem to get enough of him.

He angled his mouth against hers, exploring her lips, tasting her tongue with his, with an assertive, encompassing mastery that made Tristanne shudder with *want*. With need.

It was so carnal, so naked—and yet she remained fully clothed. His hand on the back of her neck radiated heat, and something far too like ownership. He tasted like expensive liquor and salt, intensely masculine and frighteningly addictive. Tristanne clutched at his shirt, but her hands melted against the steel-packed muscles of his chest rather than push him away.

A million years passed, a thousand ages in that same impossible fire, and then, finally, he raised his head, his dark gold eyes glittering with an edgy need. Tristanne felt the echo of it kick at her, making her legs feel weak beneath her.

She fought the urge to press her fingers to her mouth—to see how completely he had ravaged her, to feel how totally he had claimed her. Her own lips felt as if they no longer belonged to her. As if he had marked her, somehow, as his. Something inside her, low and deep, sang out at the idea.

Idiot.

She should have known better than to play such games with a man like this, a man she knew with a sudden implacable certainty, as his dark eyes bored into hers and she felt herself shiver where he still held her, she could never control. Never. She was not even sure she wanted to.

She was in terrible, terrible trouble.

She had to remember why she was doing this! She had to think of her mother first!

"I trust that was sufficient?" There was an odd light in his eyes—it made her skin draw tight and prickle in warning. He set her back from him, and drew his hand away from her nape, slowly, leaving brushfires in his wake.

She forced herself not to tremble. Not to shiver in reaction. She knew somehow that he would use her responses against her. She knew it.

"I think so," Tristanne managed to say, though her voice sounded packed in cotton wool. Her breasts were taut and full, and she longed to press them against his hard chest. It was as if he had somehow turned her own body against her. She ordered herself to stop, to breathe, to contain the hysteria.

But this was why she had chosen him. This, exactly.

"You do not know?" His full mouth curved slightly, making him look both delicious and amused. "Then I cannot have done it correctly."

Tristanne realized then that she was still touching him. Her head spun and her breath had gone shallow, but her hands still lay against the granite planes of his chest. She could feel the heat of him rise through the cloth of his shirt, and the time had long passed to let go, to step away—and yet she still held on as if he was the only thing keeping her from tilting off the edge of the world.

Get a hold of yourself! she ordered herself, desperately. She thought of Vivienne's pale, too-slender form; thought of her racking cough and sleeplessness. She had to keep her head about her, or all would be lost. *She had no choice.*

She dropped her hands. As she did so, she thought his half smile deepened, grew more darkly amused. Somehow, that made it possible for her to straighten her spine, to remember herself, remember what she must do. And for whom.

"You were perfectly adequate," she told him, trying to sound unaffected. Almost bored, even, while her heart galloped and her stomach twisted.

He did not react to her remark in any way that she could see—yet sensed a certain stillness in him, a certain focused watchfulness, that reminded her of some great predator set to pounce. The dragon, perhaps, a moment before letting loose his fire.

"Was I, indeed?" he asked coolly.

"Certainly." Tristanne shrugged as if she felt nonchalant, as if she could not feel the heat that burned in her cheeks. As if he had not turned her inside out and wrecked her completely with one kiss. One complicated, unexpected, mind-altering kiss.

But it was not the only thing she could feel. And as intoxicating as Nikos Katrakis was—as deliciously unnerving as that kiss had been—now that it was over she could also feel Peter's fury. Her brother had moved closer, and was now standing near enough that he was, no doubt, eavesdropping on her conversation with Nikos. This time, she did not look over. She did not have to—she knew exactly how Peter would be scowling at her, with that anger burning in the eyes that should have looked like hers, but were too cold, too cruel.

"Perhaps it requires further experiment," Nikos suggested, in that velvety caress of a voice that heated her from within. She put Peter out of her mind for the moment. She felt a heavy, sensual fire bloom in her core, and begin to spread outward. "I am happy to extend the favor. I would not wish to disappoint you."

"You are magnanimous indeed," she murmured, dropping her gaze—afraid, somehow, that he could see too much. That he could see exactly how much he had affected her.

"I am many things, Miss Barbery," Nikos murmured, his voice soft though his gaze, when she dared meet it, was hard. "But I am not magnanimous. I have not one generous bone in my body. I suggest you remember that."

She knew what she had to do. She had decided, even before Peter had laid out his disgusting conditions, that she was prepared to do whatever it took to emancipate her mother from Peter's control—to save her. What did she care if the Barbery fortune and financial empire collapsed into dust and ruins? She had turned her back on all of that long ago. But she could not turn her back on her poor mother, especially not now that Gustave—who her mother had loved so blindly, so foolishly—had left her so helpless and so completely under Peter's thumb. She had stayed out of it while her father lived, but she could not abandon her mother now, so frail and at risk even as she grieved for Gustave. She was all her mother had left. She was Vivienne's only hope.

Which meant she had only one course of action.

"That is a pity," Tristanne said, with a calm she did not feel. She felt panic claw at her throat, and rise like heat to her eyes, but she swallowed it. She was determined. She knew her brother was not bluffing, that he had meant every awful word that he'd said to her, that he would not rest until she *earned her keep* in service of filling the family coffers, and that he would think nothing of tossing her mother out into the street if Tristanne defied him. She knew exactly what would happen if she did not do this.

What she did not, could not know was what might become of her if she did.

"Not at all," Nikos said, his golden eyes watchful, intent. "Merely the truth."

Women do this every day, she told herself. *Since the dawn of time. With far lesser men than this.*

"It is a pity," Tristanne forced herself to say, the emotions she would not acknowledge making her voice husky, "because I had heard you were between mistresses at present. I had so hoped to be the next."

His dark eyes flared, then turned to molten gold. She held his gaze as if she were as bold, as daring, as her words suggested. Hoping that she could be. She had to be.

"But, of course," she continued, because this was the crux of it—because she knew Peter was listening, and so she had to push the words out, no matter how they seemed to clog her throat, "as your mistress, I would require your generosity. A great deal of it."

For another endless moment, Nikos only watched her, his gaze still searing through her—reducing her to ash, making her breath desert her—but otherwise his big body remained still, alert. It was almost as if she had not propositioned him. As if she had not offered to prostitute herself to him as casually as she might have ordered a drink from the bartender.

But then, making every hair on her body prickle and her nipples pull to hard, tight points, Nikos smiled.

It had been a long time in coming, this moment, and Nikos could not help but savor it. Revel in it. He had never dared dream that his arch-enemy's sister would offer herself to him, as his mistress, thus ensuring his ultimate victory—his final revenge. But he would take it—and her.

He did not have to look at Peter Barbery to feel the other man's outrage—it poured from him in waves. It felt as sweet as he had always imagined his revenge would, in all these years he'd so carefully plotted and planned, gradually drawing the noose tighter and tighter around the Barberys, forcing them ever closer to ruin.

He only wished he were not the only one left. That his critical, disapproving father, his tempestuous half sister and her unborn child, had lived to see that they had been wrong. That Nikos really would do what he'd sworn to them he would do: take down the Barberys. Make them pay. They had died hating him, blaming him; first the heartbroken Althea by her own hand and then, later, the father he had tried so hard and failed, always, to impress. But he had only used that as further fuel.

Just as he used whatever befell him as fuel. He had not allowed a childhood in the slums of Athens to hold him back, nor his mother's callous abandonment of him. When he had finally wrenched himself from the gutter, using tooth and nail and sheer stubbornness, he had not let anyone keep him from locating the father who had discarded his mother and thus him. And once he'd started to prove himself to his harsh, often cruel father, he had tried to endear himself to Althea, the legitimate, favored and beloved child. He had never resented her for her place in his father's affections, not like she had eventually blamed him, once Peter Barbery was done with her.

He looked at Tristanne, standing before him, her words still echoing in his ears as if they were a song.

He had no idea what game the Barberys were playing here, nor did he care. Did Tristanne Barbery believe she was some kind of Mata Hari? That she could use sex to control him? To influence him in some way? Let her try. There was only one person who called the shots in Nikos's bed, and it would not be her.

It would never be her. He might have felt a wild, un-precedented attraction to her—but he would take her for revenge.

"Come," he said.

He took her bare arm, relishing the feel of the supple smoothness of her bicep beneath his palm. He nodded toward the interior of the yacht, indicating his private quarters. The urge to gloat, to taunt Peter Barbery as the other man had done years ago, was almost overwhelming, but Nikos re-pressed it. He concentrated on the Barbery he had before him, the one whose scent inflamed him and whose mouth he intended to taste again. Soon.

She looked at him, but did not speak, her eyes dark—again with an emotion he could not name.

"Second thoughts?" He was unable to keep the taunt from his voice.

"You are the one who has yet to answer," Tristanne said, that strong chin tilting up, her shoulders squaring. As if she intended to fight him—as if she were already fighting him. He wanted her naked and beneath him. Now. *For revenge*, he reminded himself, *nothing more*. "Not I."

"Then it appears we have much to discuss," Nikos said.

She swallowed, the movement in the fine column of her throat the only hint she might not be as calm nor as blasé as she pretended to be. Her eyes darkened, but held his.

"You are taking me to your lair, I presume?" she asked.

"If that is what you wish to call it," he replied, amused. And powerfully aroused.

She said no more. And he made sure every eye was on them, every head was turned, her brother's chief among them, so there could be absolutely no mistake whose arm he held with such carnal possession as he led her across the deck.

Toward the master suite. Away from prying eyes—or any recourse.

Straight into his lair.

CHAPTER THREE

SHE had seen him once before.

Tristanne remembered it as if it were moments ago, when in truth it had been some ten years earlier. She walked across the crowded deck next to Nikos with her head high, her spine straight, as if she walked to her own coronation rather than to the bedroom of the man she had just offered to sleep with. For money.

But in her mind, she was seventeen again, and peering across the crowded ballroom of her father's grand house in Salzburg. It had been her first ball, and she had had too many dreams, perhaps, of waltzing beneath all the shimmering lights of the chandeliers and candles in her pretty dress. But Nikos Katrakis had not been a dream. He had strode across her father's ballroom as if it belonged to him. He had been dark and dangerous, and potent, somehow. Tristanne had not understood, then, why she was so mesmerized by the sight of him, even from afar. Why she caught her breath, and could not seem to draw a new one. Why her heart pounded in a kind of panic—and yet she could not bring herself to look away from the darkly handsome stranger who moved through her father's house as if it were his own, or ought to be.

"Who is that man?" she had asked her mother, feeling a strange, new heat move through her, along with an unfamiliar kind of shyness. It terrified her. She did not know if she wanted to run toward this oddly compelling man, or away from him.

"He is Nikos Katrakis," Vivienne had said in a soft tone. Had she also sensed his power, his magnetism? "He has business with your father, my dear. Not with you."

And now, ten years later, Tristanne still did not know whether she wished to run toward the man or away from him. She knew that his kiss was far much *more* than she had ever imagined it might be, ten years ago when she was still a girl. And she knew that his hand felt like a brand against the bare skin of her upper arm. And that she was going with him willingly. She had suggested it, hadn't she?

This was her *choice*.

He led her away from the crowd, away from the shining late afternoon sea, far into the opulent depths of the ship. Tristanne had only the faintest hectic impressions—gleaming wood and lush reception rooms, windows arching high above the dancing waves of the Mediterranean, letting in the golden Côte d'Azur light—because the only thing she could concentrate on was Nikos.

She was aware of every breath he took, every stride, every movement of the powerful body so close to hers. She could feel the hot, bright heat that seemed to burn from inside his very skin, and she knew that the heaviness in her belly, the softening below, was all for him. Her face felt red, then white, then red again, as if she was feverish.

But she knew better.

She had to get herself under control, she thought desperately. She could not lose herself in this man's touch, no matter how formidable and attractive he was. She was only using him, she told herself. He was but a means to an end.

Nikos ushered her into a room, finally, slapping the door shut behind them. Tristanne looked around, but could hardly register a thing. She had only the haziest notion that this was an elegant, spacious stateroom, and that it contained a bed. A large bed. And that she was in it, by her own design, with the most sensually dangerous man she had ever encountered.

"Mr. Katrakis," she began, spinning around to face him. It was not too late to wrest control of this situation. That was what all of this was about, in the end—control. She had only to assert herself, surely. She had only to be strong.

"It is too late for that, don't you think?" he asked, too close already, so close she could have reached out and laid her hand on that swathe of olive skin at his neck, directly in front of her eyes.

Tristanne could not help herself. She backed up a step, then froze, sure that simple reaction would give her away—would show him that she was not the sophisticated mistress sort of person she was pretending to be, that she was just an artist from Canada swept up in events outside her control. But he only smiled.

Tristanne's entire body kicked into red-alert. She felt poised on the brink of some kind of cliff, something steep and deadly, and it was as if he was the harsh, strong wind that might toss her over the side.

Dragon, she thought again. She had known it from the start—she had known it on some level ten years ago, at a distance. And yet here she was, begging to be singed. Or worse—burned to a crisp.

Nikos seemed to take over the room, as if he expanded to fill all the available space, crowding everything else out. He thrust his hands into the pockets of his denim trousers, but that in no way contained the unmistakable sensual menace he exuded like his own, personal cologne. His shoulders seemed broader, his chest wider, his height excessive. Or was it that Tristanne felt so small? So vulnerable, suddenly—completely devoid of the bravado that had carried her this far. She knew what it was now, his particular brand of potent charisma. She knew what it meant.

You must not let him shake you, she cautioned herself. *You must think only of Vivienne.*

And still he watched her with those old coin eyes, as if he was merely waiting for the right moment to pounce.

"Call me Nikos," he invited her after a moment, when the sound of her own breathing threatened to drive Tristanne to the brink.

She knew she should say something. Even, as he'd suggested, his name. But she could not form the word. It was as if she knew that once she said it, there would be no turning back. As if his familiar name was the last boundary between her old life and this new one she had to pretend to live.

And she could not seem to cross it.

His smile grew darker, more sardonic.

He leaned back against the door he'd closed, his eyes hooded. He said nothing. Then—when Tristanne's nerves were stretched to the breaking point, when she was certain she must scream, or sob, or run as her body ordered her to do, anything to break the tension—he raised his hand and crooked his finger, motioning for her to come to him.

Arrogantly. Confidently. Certain of instant obedience.

Like he was no different, after all, than men like her father and her brother.

Like she was a dog.

A sudden wild anger pulsed through her then, but she stamped it down somehow. Was that not what a mistress was, when all was said and done? A woman on command? At a man's whim? Wasn't this precisely what she'd claimed to want?

What did it matter how this arrogant man treated her? She did not, in truth, wish to become his mistress. She wanted only to make Peter think she had done it—she wanted only the appearance of this man's interest, his protection.

A few days, she had thought. What harm could truly come to her in a few short days? They would have a few dinners, perhaps share some more kisses—preferably within sight of the paparazzi who hung about the sorts of places men like Nikos Katrakis frequented. It would all be for show, and Nikos Katrakis himself need never be any the wiser.

And it was all for a good cause, lest she forget herself entirely. For her beloved, incapacitated mother, who could not seem to understand that her stepson was a monster, nor that he had no intention of caring for her as Gustave had intended. Tristanne needed access to her trust fund—which would not come to her until her thirtieth birthday, unless Peter, as executor, allowed it—so she could pay her mother's debts, see to her health and protect her from further harm. She had no choice.

So Tristanne did not laugh at Nikos, or slap him, or storm from the stateroom as she yearned to do. She was not auditioning for the role of this man's partner, much less his wife. A mistress was a mistress—and Tristanne had the feeling that Nikos Katrakis was a man who made very sure that his mistress knew her place. Instead of reacting as she wanted to, as everything in her screamed to do, she moved toward him, her hips swaying as her high heels sank into the plush carpet at her feet.

"Perhaps you should simply whistle," she could not help but say, with a bite to her tone despite the lecture she had given herself. "It will be far less confusing."

"I am not at all confused," Nikos murmured.

He straightened from the door with a lethal grace that might have dizzied her, had she had time to react. But he gave her no such courtesy. Instead he reached over and snagged her wrist with his big, strong hand, then tugged her to him as if she weighed no more than the lightest feather.

He cupped her jaw, lifting her face to meet his. It was a starkly possessive gesture, and yet, somehow, almost tender—making Tristanne gasp in confusion, and something much hotter.

Then his mouth was on hers. He spun her around until her back was against the door, and he kissed her, tasting her again and again, as if he might devour her whole.

And though she knew she shouldn't, though she knew she should think about why she was there and not her girlish fantasies of moments just like this one, she kissed him back as if she might let him—as if she might beg him. Not to let her go. But not to stop.

Never to stop.

He could not seem to get enough of her. Her sweet honeyed taste, the fit of her mouth to his, the little murmurs she made in the back of her throat, as if she could not help but respond to him with such abandon, with such passionate recklessness. Nikos felt a fire rage through him, making him hard and ready, and did not try to stop it. Could not have stopped it, even if he'd wanted to.

She wanted to be his mistress. He wanted her, with an intensity he had not expected, but had no wish to deny. He told himself that he would use it, that was all. It would merely fuel his revenge.

He pressed her back against the door, holding her there with his body while his hands roamed over her curves. One hand fisted in the dark blonde waves of her hair, tilting her head back to give him better access to her mouth, while the other stroked its way along the elegant line of her throat, then down to the sweet perfection of her jutting breasts.

Pulling away from her mouth with reluctance, Nikos turned his full attention to her breasts, tracing the flesh that swelled proudly above the bustline of her dress. He held them in his hands, weighing them against the silken material, testing their shape, running his thumbs across the hard peaks until she groaned.

It was not enough.

His blood pumped in his veins, urging him on. He reached

down and found the hem of her dress, then worked it up toward her waist, exposing her silken thighs, and the heat of her femininity between them. He pulled one long, exquisitely formed leg over his hip, settling himself against her, so his hardness was flush against her center, separated only by his trousers and a single scrap of silk. She moaned. Her hips bucked against him. Her head was thrown back against the door, her eyes closed, as if she felt the heat, the fire, as he did.

He slanted his mouth over hers, tasting her again and again, while his hips moved, rolling against hers, rocking them both toward insanity.

He buried his face in her neck, licking the hollow of her throat, while his hands found her. He cupped her heat with his palm, feeling her molten heat, her softness. She cried out. Was it his name? He found he did not care.

She was a Barbery. She was his enemy. He wanted her for revenge, and he did not yet know what she wanted from him. He only knew, in this moment, that he had to have her.

Nikos pulled her delicate, panties to one side, stroking her with his long fingers. She sobbed out words he could not identify. Then, teasing her, he circled her entrance, before succumbing to the desire he could not seem to control. She was wet, and so soft, so hot, that he had to bite back his urge to throw her to the floor and sink so deep within her that he might forget his own name. Instead he moved his hand, rocking gently against her sex—and then, not so gently.

She made a helpless sound, but then her hips began to move against his hand, riding him, as her hands clutched at his shoulders.

"Look at me," he ordered her.

Her eyes fluttered open. They were wide, and brown, and so wild with desire it made him curse. He felt her stiffen against him. She bit back a cry. Her cheeks flushed hot and red. A purely male satisfaction thrummed through him, along with a deep, primal surge of possession. He ignored it, and focused on the wet heat in his hands, the ecstasy he knew was just within her reach.

"Come for me," he whispered gruffly, pressing kisses against her mouth, her cheek, her neck. "Now."

This is a mistake, Tristanne thought in a desperate, chaotic, panicked rush—but it was too late.

Her body, tuned to his wicked fingers and not her errant thoughts, shattered into pieces at his command.

She was lost.

It took her long, shuddering moments to come back to herself. When she did, he was watching her with those dark, predatory eyes, and she did not know what she was going to do. What she *could* do, with his hand still between her legs and his mouth faintly damp from hers. She felt herself shiver in reaction. Or perhaps it was an aftershock of the explosion that had ripped through her with such strength, such fire.

One dark brow rose.

Good God, she thought with sudden, horrified comprehension, *he was not satisfied.* Of course he was not satisfied. How had she let this happen? How could she have done nothing at all to prevent it—how could she, instead, have encouraged it? She did not understand how she had lost control of the situation so quickly, so completely. She was afraid she might never understand herself again.

And why did some part of her long to simply throw caution to the wind and let him take her wherever he wished to go?

"What are we…" She was appalled to hear herself stammer out her confusion. But she could not control the tremors inside of her, the rush of conflicting emotions that buffeted her. She could not seem to avoid his knowing, faintly mocking gaze. "I did not intend…"

Her hands were braced against the wall of his chest, and she curled them into fists, as if…what? She planned to beat him off? After welcoming him into her body with such un-characteristic enthusiasm? What was *wrong* with her? She wanted to burst into tears, and she could not understand it. Everything felt too large, too unwieldy, too heavy. Her own body felt like a stranger's, humming with sensations she could not identify. She could not seem to catch her breath, and he stood so still, so close, only the barest hint of that sardonic half smile on his mouth.

He let her leg slide to the floor. Tristanne realized that her dress was still around her waist, and, flushed in an agony of shame, jerked it back into place with trembling fingers. How could she have done this? When she should be thinking only of her mother?

"Perhaps I misunderstood you," he said, his voice like velvet, though his eyes were as hard as steel. He did not back away from her. He tucked a strand of her hair behind her ear, making her choke on a breath. "I was under the impression that you wished to be my mistress. Did you not say so? What did you imagine the position entails?"

"I know what it entails," she retorted, without thinking.

"Apparently not." His mouth crooked in one corner. "Or perhaps your experience of such things differs from mine. I prefer my partners to be—"

"I am merely astounded at the speed at which you wished to consummate the relationship," she interrupted him tartly. "I do not know how things are done where you come from, Mr. Katrakis—"

"Nikos, please," he said silkily. "I know how you taste. *Mr. Katrakis* seems a bit absurd now, does it not?"

"—but I prefer a little more…" Her voice trailed away. Exactly what *did* she expect? This was…a business proposition. She had absolutely no experience to draw from, save what information she had gleaned from novels. Hardly helpful, under the circumstances.

"Wining and dining?" he finished for her. "Artifice and

pretense? I think that perhaps you do not understand the requirements here. I make the rules and demands. You do not." His head cocked slightly to the side as he regarded her with those unfathomable eyes. "Tell me, Tristanne. How many men have you been mistress to, in your glorious career?"

"What?" She was horrified, even as she shivered at the sound of her name in his wicked, talented mouth. "None!"

She should not have said that. She could have kicked herself. She might have, had he not been in the way.

"Ah, I see." That dangerous satisfaction gleamed in his gaze again. "Then why am I so lucky? What brings the heiress to the Barbery fortune to my bed, offering herself to me? I cannot make sense of such a thing."

Tristanne felt cold, suddenly; her sense of danger heightened. It was the tone in his voice, perhaps, or the way he watched her. *Remember why you are doing this,* she cautioned herself. *Remember what is at stake!*

"These are difficult times," she said with a careless sort of shrug, though she felt anything but careless. She eased away from him, moving further into the room. She was all too aware that he let her go. She did not mention that her brother was on the brink of losing the family fortune or that Peter was obsessed with Nikos and considered him his main rival and enemy. She knew, somehow, it would not be wise.

"And you are, as you know very well, a highly desirable man," she managed to say after a moment. It was no more than the truth, though perhaps the least interesting truth.

"I do not think you have the slightest idea what it means to be a man's mistress," he said from behind her, his voice soft, but with that dark current beneath.

Tristanne could not bear to look at him. She could not understand the wild tumult of emotion that seized her, that filled her eyes with tears she would rather die on the spot than shed, but she knew with perfect clarity that she could not look at him now. She could not.

"I am a quick study," she heard herself say, because she had to say something.

She heard a soft sound that could have been a low laugh, though she could not be sure.

"Turn around, Tristanne."

She did not want to. She did not know what he might see on her face—and she was certain it would only expose her further.

But this was not about her. This was about being a good daughter, for once. This was about protecting Vivienne. If she had not run off to Vancouver when her father revoked her university tuition... If she had not abandoned her mother to the tender mercies of both Gustave and Peter... But then, she had always been stronger than her mother. And now she would prove it.

She turned. He was dark and dangerous, and still as breathtaking as when she'd been seventeen. He watched her with eyes that seemed to know things about her she did not know herself, and that ever-present hint of a smile. As if she amused him. She lifted her chin, and waited.

She could do this. She would.

"This boat sails in the morning for the island of Kefallonia, my home," he told her, his velvet and whiskey voice a rough caress. His eyes gleamed with challenge. "If you wish to be my mistress, you will be on board."

CHAPTER FOUR

HE SAT at a small table on one of the yacht's decks, news-papers in three languages spread out before him and thick, rich Greek coffee within reach, basking in the morning sun-shine. The golden light poured over him, calling attention to his haughty cheekbones and the fathomless dark eyes he'd neglected to cover with sunglasses, before seeming to caress his full, wicked mouth. His long legs, encased in comfort-able tan trousers, stretched out in front of him, and he wore a linen shirt in a soft white that drew the eye, unerringly, to the hard planes of his chest and the shadow between his pectoral muscles. His feet, disarmingly, were bare.

He did not look up when Tristanne approached. She was not so foolish as to imagine, however, that he did not know she was there. She knew that he did. That he had tracked her from the moment she stepped onto this deck—perhaps even from the moment she'd climbed aboard the boat itself.

She stopped walking when she was only a few feet away, and tried to regulate her choppy, panicked breathing. She stood straight, her spine stiff and her head high. She hated herself—and him, she thought with a flash of despair, as she continued to stand there, like some supplicant before him. But she would not bow, or scrape, or whatever else she imagined a man like this must require. She would play her role—tough, sophisticated, focused entirely on what he could provide for

her. She would think of her poor mother, whose cough was
worsening and whose bills were staggering. It didn't matter,
at the end of the day, what Nikos Katrakis thought of her.
Much less what she thought of herself.

*Whoring yourself out to the highest bidder, are you? Like
mother, like daughter after all*, Peter had sneered—but she
would not think of Peter. The temptation to dissolve into
misery was far too great, and far too dangerous now. She
resisted the urge to check her smooth chignon, to run her
hands along her clothes as if her crisp white trousers and
long-sleeved, sky-blue cotton blouse might somehow have
become unkempt in the time it had taken her to board the
yacht. She could not show nervousness. She could not show…
anything, she thought, or she would crumble beneath the
pressure of what she must do.

Still, he did not glance up at her, and there was nothing to
do but stand there. She knew what he was doing—knew that
this was a casual and deliberate display of his power, that he
could and would ignore her until he saw fit to acknowledge
her presence. Whenever that might be. Her role was to take
this treatment. To ignore it, as if she often stood on the deck
of luxury yachts, listening to the sounds of surf and water
and the distant tolling of church bells, waiting for powerful
men to condescend to notice her. The events of the previous
day washed over her then and she could feel a scarlet fire
roll along the length of her body, making her stomach clench
and her breath catch. Had that really been her? That wanton
creature, so easily commanded to passion by a man she had
once dreamed might one day dance with her? Desire mixed
with shame and twisted through her stomach, but she gritted
her teeth against both.

It didn't matter what she felt. It didn't matter what had
happened, or would happen. She was here. She had put these
events into motion, and she had no choice but to see them

through. She had to think of her mother—of her mother's future.

"How long will you stand there?" Nikos asked casually, without looking up from his paper. His voice was like a touch, a rough caress that made her shiver. "Why do you loom about with that serious look on your face, as if you are attending your own execution? This cannot be how you think mistresses act, Tristanne, can it?"

Hateful man.

"I am calculating your net worth," she replied coolly. She arched her eyebrows when his old gold eyes met hers, and ruthlessly tamped down her urge to squirm, to look away, to submit to the command in even his gaze. "I imagine that is the favorite pastime of most mistresses, in fact."

His full lips twitched slightly, though he did not quite smile, as if he could not decide whether to laugh or cut her into pieces. Time seemed to fall away, as if he commanded that, too, with the power and heat in his gaze. Tristanne was aware of too many things at once, all conspiring to keep her under the spell of this dark, hard man. The golden sunshine. The lapping waves against the hull of the yacht as it moved beneath them, cutting through the swell and heading away from the French mainland. From all safety, however relative. The way his gaze touched her, heated her, for all that it was proprietary and, on some level, insulting.

"You are overlooking the primary purpose of keeping a mistress," he said softly, breaking the spell, even as he cast another with his whiskey and velvet tone. He laid his paper flat on the tabletop and leaned back against his chair, every inch of him seemingly indolent and careless. She knew better than to believe it.

"By all means," she replied evenly. She forced a smile, and reminded herself that it had been her *choice* to play this game, and there was no use being surly about it now. Vivienne was depending upon her. "Enlighten me."

He nodded at the chair next to his, a hard sort of amusement flaring in his gaze. Once again, there was no denying the command in even so small a gesture. Nor the fact that he expected instant obedience. She longed to throw it in his face with her whole heart, with every cell of her being—even as she walked slowly, casually, to the spot he had indicated and sat. Like a good, docile, well-trained girl. Like a mistress.

He was too close. He was too overwhelming. She imagined, hysterically, that she could feel the intense heat of him caressing her—even though she knew it must be the summer sun high above them. She could not seem to look away from his hands, so strong and too clever, that rested on the small table between them.

He watched as she settled herself, his lips curved into something far too cynically amused for Tristanne's comfort. His hot gaze tracked the way she folded her hands so politely in her lap, the way she sat straight in her chair, the way she crossed her legs just so—as if she was that proper, and there was no wild mess hidden beneath her surface.

As if he had not held the heat of her in his hands, and made her sob.

"Fantasy," Nikos said quietly.

Tristanne stiffened, and fought the pulsing heat that bloomed inside of her and then washed over her skin, scorching her.

"I'm sorry?" At least she did not stammer or gasp. Though she could feel a warmth behind her eyes, threatening her with complete exposure.

"A mistress's primary occupation is the spinning of fantasy," Nikos said patiently—too patiently, though Tristanne could feel the dark edge beneath. "A mistress is always ready to entertain, to soothe. She is always dressed in clothes that invite, seduce. She does not complain. She does not argue. She thinks only of pleasure." His dark eyes met hers. Burned. "Mine."

"That sounds delightful," Tristanne murmured politely. She meant to sound sultry, alluring—but just like the day before, her words somehow came out prim. Tart. "Something to aspire to, surely. With so many days at sea ahead of us, I am certain that you will find me an avid pupil of all things mistress-related."

"This is not meant to be an apprenticeship, Tristanne. I am no teacher, and I do not require a student." His dark gaze made her feel heated, restless. She thought again of mythical creatures, fairy tales. Larger than life and twice as terrifying, that was Nikos Katrakis. Just as she had dreamed long ago.

And now she was entirely within his power.

"My apologies," she said, her voice huskier than she intended. "What would you like me to do?"

"First things first," he said, his voice and gaze mocking her—daring her. "Why don't you greet me properly?" He indicated his lap with the faintest hint of a smile. "Come here."

She looked terrified—or appalled—for the barest moment, but then schooled her features with the same ruthlessness that he had seen her employ several times already. Nikos nearly laughed out loud.

Tristanne Barbery, he was certain, had about as much interest in becoming his mistress as she did in swimming across the width of the Ionian Sea with an anchor tied around her neck. And yet she rose from her seat with that quiet grace that he found uncomfortably captivating, and moved to settle herself in his lap. Somehow, she managed to do it gracefully, politely, as if seating herself on a man's lap was as decorous an activity as, say, needlepoint.

But that didn't change his body's immediate reaction, and his body was under no illusions—no matter how distant and polite she might wish to act, Nikos wanted her in every indecorous manner he could imagine. And his imagination was extraordinarily vivid.

He put his arms around her, holding her close, letting himself feel the suppleness of her skin beneath his hands and the soft cotton blouse she wore, that covered far too much of her body. He felt himself harden, instantly aroused and ready for her. It did not help that he knew exactly how soft, how hot, she would be for him. How uninhibited in passion. He let his head drop close to hers, and took a deep breath to keep himself from taking her where they sat.

It was not time. Not yet. This was about revenge, not merely sex. He did not understand why he had to keep reminding himself of that.

She wore the same sweet and spicy scent as the day before, inflaming his senses, just as she had yesterday. Her hair smelled of apples and musk, and something far more intoxicating that he suspected was all Tristanne. He dug his fingers into the sleek knot of her chignon, destroying it and its appearance of refinement, and sent her heavy mass of hair cascading down her back, enveloping them both in the scent and warmth of the dark blonde waves.

She did not say a word. She only gazed at him, her chocolate eyes shuttered; wary. She shifted against his thighs, as if nervous, moving against his arousal and then away from it, though she had little room to maneuver. She let her palms rest gingerly on the width of his shoulders, as if she was afraid to touch him.

"Much better," he said. Their faces were so close together. He could lean forward and press his mouth to the elegant column of her throat, taste that strong, determined chin. "No man likes to see his mistress looking so civilized. It borders on insult."

"I will endeavor in future to look as disreputable as possible," she said crisply. But he could feel her against him, not so restrained, her thighs restless against his. "Shall I make certain to keep my hair in a great tangle? Is that what you require?"

"That would be a good start," he said, keeping his voice serious, though he wanted to laugh. He could see the color, high and hectic, that stained her marvelous cheekbones and added a frantic sheen to her eyes, though she still held herself so rigidly against him. "But you must also do something about your clothes."

"My clothes?" she asked, stung. Her gaze narrowed on his. "What is the matter with my clothes?"

"You are dressed to meet someone's mother," he replied easily. "It is entirely too conventional and inoffensive."

"You prefer...offensive garments?" Her jaw tensed, that strong little chin lifting. "I wish you had mentioned that yesterday. I'm afraid I packed clothes more in keeping with your reputation for exquisite taste." Those challenging brows rose again. "My mistake."

"I prefer as few garments as possible," Nikos said silkily. "Exquisite or otherwise." He let one hand trail along her spine, tracing the contour of it, the shallow valley below and the ridge of it above. "Skin, Tristanne," he whispered, close to the tempting hollow of her ear, and smiled when she shivered in helpless response. "I want to see skin."

Her lips parted, though no sound emerged. Nikos smiled. She might be here for any number of reasons—and he would find her out, of that he was certain. But in the meantime, there was this chemistry between them, so surprising and electrifying. He had no intention of ignoring it. He would use it, he told himself, to make his revenge upon her—and her family—all the more devastating. It was a tool, that was all.

"When you enter a room, you must always come to me," he continued, his voice a low murmur. One hand tangled in her hair, while the other continued its lazy exploration of her back, flirting with the hem of her blouse, teasing the band of flesh exposed between the top of her trousers and the shirt's tail. "You should assume that you will sit on my lap, not your own chair, unless I tell you otherwise." He pressed his lips to the curve of her ear, then traced a pattern with his lips and tongue along the length of her fine cheekbone. She shuddered.

"I understand," she said, but her voice was the faintest whisper of sound. Her dark lashes covered her eyes, and her face was flushed. He could feel the electric current that moved through her body, making her tense and vibrate against him.

"And you should greet me, always, with a kiss," he whispered, and then took her mouth with his.

Once again, that treacherous fire swept through Tristanne, reducing her to ruins.

She was nothing but need and yearning, gasping against his mouth yet held deliciously immobile in his strong arms. She nearly forgot herself as his lips claimed hers, tangled and teased and beguiled. She *wanted* to forget herself.

But that was the one thing she must never, ever do.

Tristanne leaned back, breaking off the kiss and daring to look down at Nikos, to meet his gaze full-on. His eyes were molten gold, dark with a passionate heat that made her sex pulse in response. His mouth, so wicked and masterful, curled into the slightest of smiles.

"Thank you for the lesson," Tristanne said. Her voice was the breathiest thread of sound—completely insubstantial—and told them both far more about her frenzied state than she would ever have wished to share. How could he do this to her so easily? Some part of her had thought—hoped—that yesterday's explosive passion had been an accident of some kind—an anomaly. But this was not the time to agonize over it. There was nothing to do but brazen her way through such an unexpected obstacle.

She must not succumb to passion. Hadn't that been how her mother had thrown herself into her father's power in the first place? Tristanne would not be so stupid.

"Has it ended?" His gaze dropped from hers to trace her mouth, and his fingers spread against the exposed skin of her lower back. She fought off a shudder of reaction, but couldn't keep the heat from her face.

"Of course," she said, pretending that she could not feel the heat between them—or in any case, did not care. She leaned back slightly. *Barbery ice*, she reminded herself, with some desperation. "We already have an idea of how well we suit in this area. There are so many other areas yet to explore."

"Again, Tristanne, I believe you miss the point of the entire exercise." His voice was low, rich, amused. His midnight brows arched up, while his dark gold eyes saw far too much.

It would be so easy, Tristanne thought as she fell into that dark, honeyed gaze—too easy—to simply bend into his will. He was so powerful, so commanding, and it would be the simplest thing in the world to let herself go, and let him take control as he was, clearly, so used to doing. Hadn't yesterday showed her exactly how easy that would be? It would be like diving into the sea—the decision to dive would be the only difficult part, and everything after that would be gravity.

But who would she be then, when she had fought so hard to make a life for herself—a name for herself that borrowed nothing from her family, had nothing to do with any of them? And more important—what would become of her mother?

She thought of her mother's tears at Gustave's grave. She thought of Vivienne's forced, determined cheer in the following weeks. She thought of the fine bones on the back of her mother's delicate hand, far too visible now.

Tristanne could not acquiesce to this man, however easy it might be. *Especially* because it would be so easy to do so, and such a mistake. She had to maintain control of this situation—tenuous though it might be—or she would lose everything she had worked for over the past years, and everything she hoped for her own future and her mother's life. She had to stand up to this man, somehow—when she had chosen him precisely because he was the kind of man that no one stood up to, because no one would dare.

"Not at all," she said now, gathering her courage as best she could. She tossed her hair back from her face, and made herself smile down at him, still perched on his lap like she was sitting on a hot, iron stove. She could do this. She could hide everything she felt, and show him only what she wanted him to see. Hadn't Peter accused her of being frigid and cold a thousand times? She could pull it off. Couldn't she?

"Oh?" he asked, still so amused. Still so unmanageable, so impossible.

"While I appreciate your list of rules and regulations, and will make every effort to follow them, being a mistress is much more than the ability to follow orders." She traced the strong line of his jaw, the proud jut of his chin, with a lazy fingertip—though she felt as far from lazy as it was possible to feel. She kept on. "A good mistress must anticipate her partner's needs. She must adapt to his moods, and follow his lead. It is like a complicated dance, is it not?"

"It is not like a dance at all," Nikos replied, his eyes glittering. "Not if you are doing it correctly. Euphemism cannot change the facts, only the way they are relayed, Tristanne."

"The man is not supposed to see the steps of this dance, of course," Tristanne continued airily, as if she had such conversations regularly and they affected her not at all. "That is my job. And I do not wish to be protected from anything, I assure you. Least of all you." She lied easily, because she had no choice, and then met his gaze, hoping her own was clear, guileless. Unclouded by her own fears and indecision. "But I will confess that I am something of a perfectionist."

She shifted her weight then, leaning back so that he would

have to choose between letting her stand up or grabbing her close to his chest and making a deliberate show of his superior strength. He chose the former—though not without the faintest hint of a smirk. But Tristanne would take whatever small victories she could with this man. She knew without having to be told directly that they would be far and few between.

"By all means," he murmured, lounging back against his seat, his eyes trained on her, burning into her, "tell me more about this *job* you plan to perform with your perfectionist tendencies."

"Sex is so reductive," Tristanne said briskly. Rather than take her seat, she moved over to the nearby rail and gazed out at the sea, the passing red and gold French countryside. Her palms were damp. She could still feel the heat of him, stamped into her skin. She turned to face him, hoping she looked nonchalant.

His brows arched as he regarded her, his gaze steady. "I would imagine that depends entirely on the quality of the sex," he replied. "And with whom you are having it, yes?"

Tristanne waved a hand in the air, with a breeziness she did not feel, as if discussing sex with him was nothing to her. As if her heart did not pound heavily in her ears, her neck, her softening core. As if she could not feel a faint sheen of heat along her skin, making her too hot, too aware. *Think of your purpose here!* she ordered herself.

"There is so much more to an artful, sustained seduction," Tristanne continued, as if she had spent a significant amount of time puzzling over the issue, instead of merely last night, while she stared desperately at the ceiling in lieu of sleep and tried to come up with a plan to handle this man. She leaned back against the rail. "And that is what a mistress must do, is it not? Produce the fantasy on command. Seduce on call."

"I am glad we agree on the command and the call," Nikos

said, rubbing a finger over his chin. "It is the most important part of the equation."

"Is it?" Tristanne let out a trill of laughter, and immediately regretted it. The laughter was too much—too absurdly blasé. It gave her away, surely. But he only watched her, much the way large and deadly predators watched their prey before making a quick meal of them. *He is a dragon*, she reminded herself, and she already felt as if she had the burn marks to prove it. Blisters everywhere he'd touched her. She could almost feel them on her skin.

"It is to me," Nikos said after a moment. "This conversation is missing the crucial point, I think. I am delighted that you wish to perform well as my mistress. But if you think that there is some debate, some contention, over who is in charge of the relationship, I must disabuse you of the notion at once."

He did not need to deepen his tone, or strengthen the force of his dark gaze when he said such things and, indeed, he did not. He actually relaxed. He lounged in his chair, and stretched out his long legs. He spoke casually, almost as if what he said was an afterthought.

But his undisputable power hummed in the air between them, making the fine hairs on the back of Tristanne's neck stand at attention.

"You are misunderstanding me," Tristanne said in the soothing, conciliatory tone she used primarily with her mother when Vivienne was inconsolable, from her ailments or her grief. When that maddening half smile of his deepened, she knew he recognized exactly what sort of tone it was. That it was meant to handle him, appease him.

"I doubt that very much," he said. "But, of course, I did not have the benefit of your expensive education. Perhaps you must explain things to me in very small and simple words, so that I will understand you."

Tristanne did not address the idiocy of that remark, though

the hard gleam of something like bitterness in his eyes was momentarily disconcerting. She shook it away. In a week's time, she would be on her way back to Vancouver with her trust fund and her mother, and whatever bitterness he carried within him would remain his and his alone. It was no concern of hers.

"I am trying to point out to you that we must concentrate on things other than sex," she said matter-of-factly, pushing away the odd urge to ask him what he meant about his education, or hers. "Sex is easy, but seduction requires more flair, does it not? If I am to serve you well, I must access your brain as well as your body. All good seductions begin with the brain, and only use the body as something secondary. A dessert, if you will."

"My brain," he repeated. He shook his head. "*My brain* is not the part of me that invited you on to this yacht, Tristanne."

"It should have been," she replied. She met his gaze again, and then there was nothing left but to go for it. "Because we cannot have sex, Nikos. Not so soon. Certainly not on this boat."

CHAPTER FIVE

HE LAUGHED.

It was a bold, bright sound. It took Tristanne by surprise, and seemed to ring inside of her like some kind of bell. She had to remind herself to breathe, to keep herself from laughing with him—it was that compelling.

"Why am I not surprised by this turn?" he asked. Rhetorically, obviously. Still laughing slightly, his teeth gleaming white and his eyes like rich honey, he met her gaze. "Explain to me, please, why I would consent to such a thing?"

"I've just explained it to you," Tristanne replied, trying to maintain the air of insouciance she had managed to use like a shield so far.

"So you have." He shook his head slightly. Then shrugged. "If that is what you want, then what is it to me?" His tone was light, his eyes anything but.

She was so consumed by that hard, hot gaze that she almost didn't hear him. Then, when his words penetrated, she thought for a long moment that she had misheard him. Had he...agreed?

"What does that mean?" she asked when he did not speak again.

"You may set whatever limits you like," he said easily. Again, that careless shrug that only called attention to the muscles that moved, lithe and dangerous, beneath his skin. "You need only mention that they have been reached, and I will not argue."

For a moment, she watched him, caught by his potent masculinity in ways she was afraid to examine. Far above, a gull called, then dropped in a graceful arc toward the beckoning sea.

"That is not quite the same thing as agreeing, I cannot help but notice," she said, when the odd hush around them made her too restless to remain silent any longer.

"No." His half smile appeared again, mocked her. "It is not."

"I really feel that we must come to some kind of—"

"We will not come to an agreement," he interrupted her smoothly, unapologetically. He rose then, in a show of graceful, careless strength, and moved toward her, blocking out her view of the Mediterranean, the sun, the world. He reached across the scant space between them, and tugged on a stray strand of her hair. It was an oddly affectionate gesture, for all that it was also a naked display of possession.

"I will not promise you such a thing. I will only promise you that if you do not wish it, you need only say so. Isn't that enough?"

It would be enough if he were any other man alive, Tristanne thought with no little bitterness. She had never had any trouble at all before, because she had never combusted before at a man's slightest touch. She had never had to *remind herself* of all the reasons why she could not simply surrender herself to a man's fire; she had instead had to come up with reasons why she should bother to go on a second date or return a telephone call.

"It is a start," she said eventually, feeling mutinous as she looked at him.

"If it helps," he said softly, still far too close, his hands coming to rest on either side of her, caging her against the boat's rail, "I believe in a more holistic approach. Mind and body as one. You might wish to incorporate that into your seduction plans."

"A good seduction does not simply *happen*," Tristanne retorted, aware that her voice sounded cross, when, once again, she'd wanted to appear effortless. Easy. "It requires a certain amount of research, of mystery, of planning—"

"Of this," he said. He bent and nipped gently at her chin, then pressed his lips to hers. It was not the consuming kiss of before, but it was no less demanding. It was like a brand. A stamp of ownership. Of intent.

He pulled back, and laughed again, more softly this time. Then he let his hand drop down, tracing a path from her neck, across her collarbone toward her shoulder, and then squeezed the bicep that he had held yesterday.

She tried to control her immediate wince of pain, but knew she failed when his dark eyes narrowed. He released her immediately.

"That hurt you?" He frowned.

"No," she lied, shame twisting through her, cramping her stomach. "It was a sudden chill, I think…"

But he ignored her, and drew the billowing sleeve of her shirt up along the length of her arm. Tristanne did not know why she simply stood there and let him do it, as if he had somehow mesmerized her into compliance. But she did.

He muttered something harsh in Greek, and stared at her upper arm. Tristanne knew what he would see—she had seen the livid marks after her shower this morning, red and blue and black. One for each of Peter's fingers.

She felt a rush of that toxic cocktail of shame, rage and fear that always flooded her when Peter's aggression came out—and when it was noticed. When she was forced to explain that this was how her only sibling treated her. She felt that blackness roll through her, tears much too close—

"It is nothing," she said in a low voice, and then, finally, jerked away from him, pushing her sleeve back down. She tilted her chin up, not sure what she would do now. What she would do if she saw even the faintest hint of pity in those dark gold eyes where there had been so much heat—

But his gaze was unreadable. He only watched her for a long moment, and then stepped away from her in one of those impossibly graceful movements that took her breath away and in the same instant reminded her of how dangerous he was.

"I must tend to some business affairs," he told her, towering over her. She told herself that it was the simple fact of his height that made her feel so small, so vulnerable—not what he had just seen. Not what he now knew, that she had never meant to share. "I suggest that you slip into something significantly more revealing and enjoy your indolence. We will dock this evening in Portofino."

He sent her another long, intense, unreadable look, and paused for a moment. A shadow moved across his face, and she thought he might speak, but it passed as quickly as it had come. He turned and walked away without another word, leaving her to the tumult of her own thoughts.

A proper mistress would have availed herself of the opportunity to flaunt her wares, Nikos thought later that afternoon as he concluded another in a long series of tedious phone conferences with business associates in Athens who could not, apparently, follow simple instructions. A malady that was going around.

An enterprising mistress might have indulged in topless sunbathing, perhaps. Or in the lengthy and comprehensive application of unnecessary lotion while in deliberately provocative poses, having known full well that he was watching. A mistress would have known that a day on a yacht was meant to be spent securing her position, and the best way to achieve that was to make certain her every word and deed served to arouse her protector.

Tristanne Barbery, yet again, proved that she had no concept at all of what made a decent mistress. She had spent the entire day with her face pressed into a novel. A large, heavy paperback, with exceedingly dense and small print. The sort of novel that announced its reader *had thoughts*. Deep and complex thoughts, no doubt, which no man sought in his mistress—as she might look to share those deep and complex thoughts with him when he wished only to be soothed and eased and pampered. Still, the book might have been marginally acceptable had she been wearing something appropriate to her station. A miniscule bikini, perhaps, to soak in the Mediterranean sun. One of those gauzy so-called coverups that clung to each curve and begged to be removed. But Tristanne, despite what he had told her earlier, quite clearly, he'd thought, had not changed her clothes.

He would assume she was defying him, deliberately, had he not had the lowering suspicion that she was genuinely caught up in her reading and had forgotten him entirely.

He had no earthly idea why he found her so entertaining, when she was meant to be no more than the key to his revenge. The means to a long overdue end.

"Arketa," he said into the telephone now. *"Teliosame etho."*

He did not need to give the conversation more than a shred of his attention to know that it should end, and now. After some back and forth regarding the details of a particular contract he had expected to have signed weeks before, he finished the call. He rubbed his hands over his face, leaning back in the great leather chair that sat behind the highly polished wood of his desk. He knew that if he turned around and looked out the window, he would see Tristanne as she had been for hours now—curled up on one of the bright white loungers beneath an umbrella out on the deck, her attention entirely focused on the book in her hands.

But he did not need to turn, because the image was already

seared into his brain. Why should he find her so arousing? So amusing? Why did he feel a smile on his own lips, even now, when he was alone?

His reaction to her was unusual. He had never experienced anything like it—it was intriguing as much as it was unwelcome. He had had women who fulfilled every last "requirement" he had laid out for Tristanne this morning. Many of them. And none of them had interested him half as much as this one, who was, if today was any indication, shaping up to be, quite possibly, the worst mistress of all time.

He turned without meaning to do so, and sure enough, she was still in the same position on the plush lounge chair. Her knees were pulled up, and she frowned as she read, oblivious to the world around her—and to his gaze from the window above. Her dark blonde hair was back in another forbidden twist, though strands flew free in the breeze from the ocean, and she nibbled gently on one finger with that lush mouth of hers that he was not nearly done with, not yet. He felt desire pulse in his sex, low and insistent.

He wondered what game she thought she was playing, still. Did she think she would win it? Did she imagine that Nikos Katrakis was the posturing, toothless dog that her brother was? She would learn soon enough that he could not be leashed.

His mood darkened immediately at the thought of Peter Barbery—but not, for once, with thoughts of the damage Peter had wrought so long ago on what had passed for Nikos's family. Instead he thought only of those bruises on Tristanne's otherwise flawless flesh—bruises he had no doubt whatsoever Peter had put there.

He was surprised at the smoldering rage that rolled through his gut, and the possessive edge to it that fanned it on. It was no more than any man must feel when faced with evidence that another of his sex was no better than an animal, he told himself resolutely. He did not prey upon the weak and innocent like Peter Barbery.

Except for Tristanne—

But he did not allow himself to finish the thought, because it was impossible. Tristanne Barbery, sister of his sworn enemy, had not walked up to him and demanded he kiss her in front of some seventy witnesses by divine accident. She had had an agenda from the first—one that was very obvious to Nikos, for all that she tried to weave her desperate webs to conceal it. She had no interest in the role she'd claimed to want, and no talent for it, either. Nikos didn't know yet what she did want, but he did know that the fact she was not what she claimed to be meant she could not possibly be an innocent in all of this. She could not.

She was a Barbery. How could anything else matter? She was a Barbery—and that was all Nikos needed to know. That was all there was to know.

She might entertain him in a way he had not imagined a woman could, but that was of no matter. He might want her in a way he had not expected, but then, he had never been one to deny his appetites, no matter how inconvenient. He could use all of that for his own ends.

It would in no way prevent him from taking his revenge.

"Tell me," Nikos said that evening, his low voice making the fine hairs all over Tristanne's body stand at attention. "Does your brother often leave his mark upon your skin?"

It was the first time he had spoken since they'd left the yacht, and his voice seemed to echo off of the cobblestone street around them, ricocheting off of the famous yellow and pink pastel buildings of Portofino that clustered in a sparkling curve around the pretty, tiny harbor, and stood out against the green hills of pine, cypress and olive that rose steeply behind them. Or perhaps she only thought so, as she flexed her bruised arm slightly in response and felt that twist of shame roll through her again. That deep, black despair.

Tristanne took a quick breath to dispel it, and snuck a glance at the striking man who walked so quietly, so deliberately, at her side. His mood had changed considerably over the course of the day. Gone was the mockery and the sly insinuations; the man who met her for dinner after the sun had set in a red and orange inferno above the turquoise sea was quiet and watchful now. Brooding. He walked beside her with his hands thrust into the pockets of his dark trousers, a crisp white shirt beneath his expertly tailored jacket, which hugged the contours of his broad, muscled shoulders intimately.

"Of course not," Tristanne said. She was surprised to hear her own voice sounded so hushed, as if she expected to hear it tossed back from the hills, her lie repeated into every passing ear. She frowned at her feet, telling herself that she was concentrating on walking in her high, wedged sandals over such tricky, ancient ground. That was all. That was the only reason she felt so unsettled, so unbalanced.

She wished she had not dressed for him. She wished even more that she did not know perfectly well that she had done so. At first she did not understand how she had found herself in this particular dress, an enticing column of gold that reminded her of his eyes. It poured over her curves from two delicate wisps of spaghetti straps at her shoulders and swished enticingly around her calves as she moved. She did not know why she had left her hair down, so that it swirled around her upper arms and her naked back, nor why she had dabbed scent behind her ears and between her breasts, so that it breathed with her as she moved. Why she had so carefully outlined her eyes with a soft pencil, or why she had darkened her lashes with a sooty mascara. It was as if someone else, some other Tristanne, had done those things, made those choices.

Until she had walked out onto the deck, and seen him, and then she'd known exactly what she'd been doing, and why. That knowledge poured into her, filling her and washing through her, nearly making her stumble as she walked. Her motivations were suddenly as clear to her as if she'd written them out in a bullet-point list. As if they were glass. It had been all for that quicksilver gleam in his eyes when he looked around from his position at the railing and saw her. That sudden flare of heat in his old coin eyes, quickly shuttered.

And what did that make her, already far too susceptible to the one man to whom she could never, ever surrender herself? What in the world did she think she was doing with him— when she should have thought of nothing but her necessary goal? Her poor mother? She should have dressed in sackcloth and ashes—anything to repel him.

But she did not wish to repel him, a traitorous voice whispered. Not really. Perhaps not at all. She pulled her wrap closer around her shoulders, and frowned intently at the cobblestones beneath her feet as they made their way along the harborside quay toward the bustling center of the small village.

"That is all you have to say?" Nikos asked, a certain tenseness in his voice. Tristanne looked at him then, no less imposing in the soft, Italian night than he was in the stark light of morning.

"Must I defend my family?" she asked, with a casual sort of shrug that she did not feel. She had perfected it over the years, to deflect exactly this kind of attention. "All families have their little skirmishes, do they not? Their bad behavior and regrettable scenes?"

"I am no expert on families," he said, with a derisive snort. "But I am fairly certain most restrain themselves from physical displays of violence. Or should."

"I bruise very easily," Tristanne murmured dismissively. Better Peter should take out his rage on her than on Vivienne,

Tristanne thought, as she always had. She did not want to think about the way Peter's fingers had dug into her flesh, nor the words he had thrown at her, his face contorted in fury. And she did not want to talk about this. Not with Nikos. Not ever. She felt the punch of something edgy and heavy in her gut, but she struggled to repress it.

Not now, she ordered herself fiercely, blinking back the heat behind her eyes. *Not with him. It does not matter what I dreamed of when I was seventeen—he can be nothing to me!*

Nikos stopped walking, and she did, too, turning toward him warily. He stood with his back to the famous Piazzetta, the faint breeze from the water playing through his thick, black hair. His gaze was dark, troubled.

"What kind of man is your brother, that he would put his hands on you in this way?" he asked, condemnation ringing in his voice. "Surely your father would not have countenanced such behavior, were he still alive."

It was the *certainty* in his voice that did it, somehow. It was all…too much. Tristanne flushed hot with that toxic mixture of shame and fury, and it was all directed at the man who stood there before her, beautiful and disapproving in the lights that spilled from the restaurants that lined the Piazzetta.

It was all his fault! He was beguiling when he should have disgusted her, and she hated that he knew what Peter had done. That he knew exactly how little her own brother thought of her. What did that say about her? About how worthless her own brother found her?

And what did it say about her that she cared what this man thought about it? About her? When his thoughts should not matter to her at all?

"What kind of man is Peter?" she asked, her temper kicking in again, harder, and scalding her from within. At least it was better than tears. Anything was better than tears. "I don't know how to answer that. A typical man? A normal man? They are all more or less the same, are they not?" She felt wild, as if she careened down a narrow mountain pass, out of control and reckless.

The elegant arch of his dark brows did nothing to stop her. "Careful, Tristanne," he said softly, but she did not wish to be careful.

"They control. They demand. They issue orders and care not at all for the feelings or wishes of anyone around them." She threw her words at him like blows, for all the good it did her. He did not move. He did not flinch. He only stared at her with eyes that grew darker by the second. And still she continued. "They crush and flatten and maim as they see fit. What is a little bruise next to everything else a man is capable of? Next to what *you* are capable of, for that matter?"

It seemed as if the world stopped turning. As if nothing existed save her labored breathing and the sounds of *la dolce vita* all around, spilling out of the cafés and trattorias and somehow failing to penetrate the tense, tight bubble that surrounded them.

She did not want to feel this way. She wanted to play her part the way she'd planned—bright and easy and seductive— and instead she kept tripping herself up on her own jagged emotions. Was it him? Was he the reason she could not control herself the way she wanted to—the way she had prided herself on doing the whole of her adult life? Her control had saved her in tense interactions with her family—why couldn't she summon it now?

Nikos did not move, and yet he seemed to loom over her, around her, filling her senses and her vision. Filling the whole universe with his smooth muscles, his dangerous mouth, his molten gold eyes with that hard edge within. Just as she feared he would do. Just as she knew he would.

He reached over and brushed her hair back from her face with a gentleness that belied the tension she could feel shimmering between them, then followed a long strand down toward her neck, pulling it between his fingers as if he could not quite bear to let it drop. His mouth moved as his hand returned to his side, but then he shook his head slightly, as if thinking better of whatever he had been about to say.

A couple strolled too close to them on the narrow quay, almost jostling into Tristanne. But Nikos shot out a hand again and moved her out of the way, his touch shocking against her skin for all that it was protective, even kind. He did not speak, but he did not drop his hand from her forearm, either. Tristanne imagined she could see the force of his touch, the feel of it, dancing over her like light, illuminating all of her hidden places, her shadows.

She could not do this. Any of this. She could not *feel*. Neither temper nor despair nor…this softer, scarier thing she dared not name. Emotion had no place here, between them. She could not allow it.

She cleared her throat. "I am speaking rhetorically, of course," she said, her voice husky with the things she could not show, not even to herself.

"Of course."

His mouth flirted with that half smile of his that she was appalled to realize she wanted to see, even *yearned* to see, while his eyes gleamed almost silver in the dark. She shivered, though she was not cold.

"Come," he said quietly. "It is time for food, not fighting."

CHAPTER SIX

NIKOS did not understand how he could possibly have rowed in a public street. With a woman he had yet to take to his bed, no less. It defied all reason. It went against nearly forty years of habit and precedent, for that matter, and disturbed him deeply.

He was not in the habit of suffering through emotional scenes, his own or anyone else's. He did not soothe hurt feelings or tactfully contain angry explosions. He had never before entertained the faintest urge to do either. He did not allow emotion into his life, in any form. Not anymore. It had been long years since he'd backed down from a challenge or left accusations unanswered—in fact, he preferred to respond as forcefully as possible, decimating his accusers, grinding them into dust beneath his feet, ensuring neither they nor anyone in their vicinity would dare to test him again.

Until tonight.

He sat across from Tristanne in his favorite waterfront trattoria, the light from a hundred flickering candles playing over her lovely features, wondering what spell she had cast upon him to make him behave so unlike himself. He paid no attention to the fine, fresh food before them—airy foccacia with a tangy olive tapenade, hand-crafted pasta flavored with *pesto corto*, grilled peppers and anchovies, and the freshest fish imaginable tossed with garlic and olive oil. How could he concentrate on food? He was galled by his own uncharacteristic display of something very close to weakness. The worst kind of weakness—and to a Barbery, no less!

Was that her game? To make him betray his own vows to himself? If so, he was appalled to see how well it was working. What was next? Would he break into sobs in the center of the village piazza? Weep for his wounded inner child? He would more readily saw off his own head with the butter knife that rested on the crisp white linen tablecloth before him.

"You are by far the most mysterious member of your family," he said, because that was the point, after all, of this charade, was it not? To destroy the Barberys by whatever means necessary, to gather the information he needed to do so? More than this, he needed to break the silence. Quiet between them seemed too dangerous now; too fraught with undercurrents and meanings he refused to explore. Sexual tension he understood, even encouraged. Anything beyond that was anathema to him. He was here to seduce her, to wreak his revenge on her very skin—not to *comfort* her.

"Mysterious?" He noticed the way she tensed in her chair. Did she expect an attack? Perhaps she should. Her eyes met his briefly. "Hardly."

It made it worse, somehow, that she looked so beautiful. Still not the obvious, provocative beauty of a proper mistress, but rather her own potent brand of bewitching femininity that seemed to go straight to his head—and his groin. She looked too good for a sewer rat like him, far too pedigreed and finished and perfected. She was all gold and class and melted chocolate eyes—the kind of woman he would have yearned for heedlessly in his desperate youth, knowing his hands would only dirty her, ruin her, destroy her in the very act of worshipping her. He almost hated her for reminding him of those terrible days, when he'd still operated blindly from his rage, his agonized determination to escape, rather than the cool analytical mind and sharp business acumen he relied on as an adult.

But he was no longer that child. He had exorcised that particular demon, and any outward expression of his darkest rage, many years ago.

"Your father and brother and even your mother have been seen in all the halls of Europe over the past decade," he said simply, ignoring the unacceptable mix of chaos and desire that surged within him, focusing on his purpose. "You have not. One began to imagine you were merely a legend. A fairy story of the lost Barbery heiress."

She gazed at him for a moment, then returned her attention to her plate. "I was not lost." She smiled then, that excessively polite curve of her mouth that put him instantly on alert. "My father and I had a difference of opinion regarding my course of study at university. I chose to follow my own path."

"What does that mean?" he asked. He was caught by the way the candlelight made her skin glow like rich, sweet cream above the warm golden caress of her gown. He blinked. She did not appear to notice his fascination.

"It means that I chose to pursue a Fine Arts degree, even though my father felt that was a waste of time. He thought Art History would be more appropriate—better suited to cocktail party conversation with potential husbands." Tristanne toyed with her fork—nervously, he thought, and then finally set it down against her plate. "I wanted to draw, you see. To paint."

That simply, she reminded him of who they were, and why they were here. Nikos had never had the luxury of indulging the creative impulse—he had been far too busy fighting for survival. And then, when survival was assured, making certain that he would never again even approach destitution, or anything like it. Drawing? Painting? That was someone else's life. Not his.

"That is not very practical," Nikos said, unable to keep

the bite from his tone. "Is that not the point of university? Practicality? An education in service of your future?"

"You would have gotten on well with my father," Tristanne said dryly. She shifted in her seat, the candlelight caressing her cheeks, her neck, the hint of velvety shadows between her breasts. "When I opted to ignore his advice, he retracted my funding. I decided to move to Vancouver, which, apparently, sent him into apoplexy, as my father did not care to be defied." She smiled slightly. "None of this made for pleasant family reunions, so you will understand why the halls of Europe were without me for so long."

There was a subtle mockery in her tone. He ignored it.

"I trust you do not cast yourself as the victim in this scenario," he said, his voice like a blade. "Those who accept financial support cannot whine about their loss of independence. About feeling *crushed* or *flattened*. Everything comes at a price."

He expected a storm of emotion—tears, perhaps; a repeat of what had occurred in the piazza. But Tristanne only held his gaze, her own surprisingly clear, if narrowed.

"I do not disagree," she said after a moment. "I am not, I think, the hypocrite you would prefer me to be. I chose not to accept any financial support whatsoever from my father once I moved to Canada."

Something he could not identify moved through him. He called it anger. Distaste. And yet he knew it was not that simple—or, perhaps, it was not directed across the table.

"You *chose*?" he echoed. "Or were you disowned?"

"Who can say who disowned who?" Tristanne replied in a light tone he did not quite believe. "Either way, I never took another cent from him." Her chin tilted up; with pride, he thought. He felt a stab of recognition, and ruthlessly suppressed it. "I may have to wait tables or tend a bar, but it's honest work. I don't have much in Vancouver, but everything I do have is mine."

He could not have said what he felt then, staring at her, but he told himself it was a simmering rage. They were not at all similar, despite her words. Her pride. For what was she really but one more spoiled heiress who made the usual noises about her independence, but only so far as it suited her? She had come running back to Europe quickly enough after Gustave had died, hadn't she? Did she hope to get into her brother's good graces now that he controlled the purse strings? What did she know about real struggle, about truly fighting for something, anything, to call one's own because the alternative was unthinkable?

Not a damn thing.

"How noble of you to abandon your considerable fortune and fight for your preferred existence by choice rather than necessity," Nikos drawled, and had the satisfaction of watching her pale. His smile could have drawn blood. He wished it did. "The desperate residents of the slums where I grew up salute you, I am sure. Or would, if they could afford to have your exalted standards."

He had the pleasure of watching her flush red, though she did not otherwise change expression. She met his gaze steadily, as if she was not afraid of him, when he knew better. He had seen to it that she was. Or should be. And he knew that she should be.

"And, of course, those standards no longer apply," he said smoothly, daring her to continue defying him. "Since you are here. My brand-new mistress, who has such high hopes for my *generosity*. Did the charms of honest work pale, Tristanne? Did you remember that you need not work for your money after all?"

"Something like that," she bit off.

Her gaze dropped then, and her hands trembled slightly, and he told himself he was glad. Because this was how it had to be between them, no matter how much he desired her, and how he planned to indulge that desire. She was payback, nothing more.

He was certain of it.

Tristanne was still smarting from that conversation and the unpleasant emotions it had stirred up within her the following afternoon, some two hundred kilometers to the south and east in Florence.

Their strained evening in Portofino had led to a long, sleepless night aboard the yacht. For her, in any event. Tristanne had tossed from side to side in her stateroom's large, unfamiliar bed as the hours ticked by, growing increasingly more frustrated as the night wore on into morning. Had part of her been waiting, wondering if Nikos would come to her as she'd thought he might—to assert whatever "rights" he believed he had over her? She was supposed to be his mistress, after all, and he had made it clear he intended that relationship to be sexual upon his command—which, she told herself firmly, made her despise him. *That*, clearly, was the source of the burning restlessness that had her nerves stretched thin, her skin too sensitive to the touch.

Or had she simply been too agitated from all that he had said to her—and, worse, all that she had felt? Why should she feel anything at all, she had asked herself again and again throughout the night? Why should she care what he thought, especially about her, when he was nothing but smoke and mirrors, a trick, to make Peter do as she wished?

Not that any of it had mattered, in the end. She had fallen into a dreamless sleep just as the night sky began to bleed into blue through her porthole. She had not wanted to wake for the breakfast Nikos had told her, curtly, would be at half past nine—but she had. She had taken a very long, very hot shower in an attempt to conceal her exhaustion, and yet when she'd found him in the boat's lavish receiving room, Nikos had barely spared her a glance.

"Be ready in thirty minutes," he had said without looking up from his high-tech PDA, Greek coffee steaming at his elbow. "We must go to Florence."

"Florence, *Italy*?" Tristanne had asked. She'd shaken her head in confusion or exhaustion, or some combination thereof. "I thought we were going to Greece." She had stared at the plentiful breakfast buffet spread out before her on the rich wood table, bright and colorful fruits, fluffy egg dishes, flaky, perfect pastries—and, for some reason, all of it had seemed completely unappealing.

He had looked at her then, his dark eyes hard and that full mouth unsmiling. She had had to order herself not to react, not to shiver, not to give in to the command in that searing gaze.

"Be ready," he said again, his voice low, his tone ruthless, "in thirty minutes."

She had taken forty minutes—her own quiet protest—which he had assiduously ignored. He had continued to ignore her. He had taken several calls as they walked into the village of Portofino again, barking out orders in emphatic Greek as they climbed the hill away from the piazza where, she had been ashamed to remember, she had so betrayed herself the night before.

He had handed her into the gleaming black, low-slung Italian sports car that awaited them at a private garage, and had not bothered to make conversation with her as he drove. Tristanne told herself she did not care what he did; it did not matter. Nikos drove as he did everything else—with ruthless command and a complete disregard for others. She had stared out the window as the powerful car hugged the craggy coastline, her eyes drinking in the Italian sea spread out below her, sparkling in the morning light. It was mesmerizing, turquoise and inviting, and she'd wanted to be out of that car and as far away from the dark, grim driver beside her as the sea could take her. She must have drifted off to sleep at some point, for when she woke, it was to find herself deep in the heart of Florence.

The city was a hectic blur of russet-topped stone buildings and narrow, medieval streets; the Tuscan hills rising serene and green in the distance, the gleaming waters of the wide River Arno welcoming and yet mysterious as it cut through the city. Yet the city seemed strangely distant for all that it was right there on the other side of the car window. It was the man beside her, she realized as she came fully awake. He was like some kind of electrical source, emanating heat and power with such force that even the jewel of the Italian Renaissance seemed to fade when he was near.

You must still be dreaming, she told herself sharply now, as the car purred around a tight corner, low and muscular. *Wake up!*

"How long was I asleep?" she asked, her voice sounding much too loud in the close confines of the car. Had she really fallen asleep in this man's presence? She could only blame her sleepless night—surely, only exhaustion could possibly have allowed her to lower her walls so completely. Her hands moved to her hair involuntarily, as if smoothing it back into place might ease her sudden acute embarrassment that he had seen her in so defenseless a state.

"I stopped counting your snores some time ago," Nikos responded dryly. "Musical as they were."

She shot him a look, and saw that half smile of his playing over his mouth. She could not imagine what it might mean—or why she interpreted it as softer, somehow. She knew better. She knew any softness from this man was momentary at best, like a trick of the light.

"I do not snore," she said, her voice sharper than she meant it to be. She cleared her throat, and forced herself to relax, at least outwardly. "How rude!"

"If you say so," he replied. His dark gaze swept over her for a brief, electric moment, then returned to the road in front of him. "But I think it is far ruder to fall asleep in someone else's presence. I am wounded that you find me so profoundly boring, Tristanne."

Intuition—and the suicidal urge to poke at him—made her smile like a cat with a bowl of cream. Perhaps she thought she was dreaming, and that he could not harm her. Awake, she should have known better.

"Poor Nikos," she said with bright, false sincerity. "This must have been a new experience for you. I am sure the women of your acquaintance normally go to great lengths to pretend that you are so captivating, so *interesting*, that they can scarcely breathe without your express permission. Much less sleep." She made a show of yawning, and stretched her feet out in front of her, as if she was not in the least bit captivated, interested, or even aware of his brooding presence beside her.

She was dimly aware that the car stopped moving, but she could hardly concentrate on something so minor when he was turning toward her, his big body dwarfing the sleek confines of the car's leather interior, his dark eyes glittering with something edgy and wild that she could not identify.

Though her body knew exactly what it was, and hummed in sensual response, her breasts growing heavy and her nipples hardening beneath the simple green knit sheath she wore.

"Once again," he said, his voice smooth and dangerous, "I am astonished at how little you seem to know about being a man's mistress, Tristanne. Do you truly believe that my former mistresses taunted me? *Mocked* me?"

Some demon took her over, perhaps, or it was that restlessness inside of her that made her ache and burn and *need*. But she did not—could not—cower or apologize or back down at all, despite the clear sensual menace in his voice, his gaze, the way his arm slid along the back of her seat and hemmed her in, caged her, *reminded* her of the role she was supposed to be playing.

Whatever it was, she met his gaze. Boldly. Unapologetically. As if this was all part of her plan. She raised her brows, challenging him.

"And how quickly did you tire of them, I wonder?" she asked softly, directly. "So accommodating, so spineless. Do you even remember their names?"

Something too primal to be a smile flashed across his face then. His eyes turned to liquid gold, like a sunset across water, and Tristanne forgot how to breathe.

"I will remember yours," he promised her. "God help you." He let out a sound too harsh to be laughter, and nodded toward her window, and through it toward the covered archway that led to the imposingly large door of the ancient-looking building before them. "But there is no time for this now. We have arrived."

She could not say if she was relieved or disappointed when he left her scant moments after he ushered her into the sumptuous foyer of the sprawling flat. It commanded the whole of the top floor of an old building tucked away on an ancient side street in the city center. Tristanne did not realize how central it was, in fact, until the door closed behind Nikos and she turned to gaze out the floor-to-ceiling windows that comprised the far wall. She was staring directly at the famous red and marble dome of the cathedral of Santa Maria del Fiore itself. Brunelleschi's world-renowned Duomo was the whole of the view—filling the wall of windows and so close she felt as if she could very nearly reach out and touch it.

Naturally this would be where Nikos Katrakis kept an extraordinarily sumptuous flat he could not possibly use very often. It was an architectural feat—high, graceful ceilings and a loft's sense of space inside a historical building dating back to the Middle Ages. *Of course* he simply kept such a place as his Florentine pied-à-terre.

Tristanne had grown up with wealth; had been surrounded by it for all but the last few years of her life. And still, the cold calculation necessary to make and maintain such wealth remained breathtaking to her, even shocking—the reduction of everything, anything, *anyone* to little more than currency, items to be bought, hoarded, sold, or bartered. Tristanne's father had been that kind of man. Cold. Assessing. Moved by money alone, and sentiment? Emotion? Never.

Nikos had not even glanced at the stunning view that would no doubt transport the sea of tourists who swarmed the city daily into raptures. The Duomo was one of the foremost sights in Italy, in the world. It was internationally, historically significant. And yet he had given a few curt orders to his staff, informed Tristanne he had meetings he expected to return from no later than six in the evening, and had then left. Had he bought this flat because he loved this view and wished to gaze at it whenever he happened to be in Florence? Or had he acquired it simply because it made good business sense as an investment property—because it had one of the most desirable and thus most expensive views in the whole city?

"You are leaving?" she had asked, surprised, when he'd turned to go. "And what am I to do for all of these hours?"

He had looked almost affronted by the question. "What mistresses always do, I would imagine," he had replied in that silken tone. He'd crooked his brow. "Wait. Prettily."

Wait. Prettily. Like a seldom-used property. Had that not been what Tristanne's mother had done her entire life?

She moved closer to the windows now, something like sadness seeming to suffuse her, to swallow her whole, though she could not have said why. She did not know how long she remained in that same position, staring unseeing at the glorious marble and distinctive red tiles before her. She felt a sudden, sharp pang of homesickness stab at her. She wanted to be back in her cheerful little apartment in the Kitsilano neighborhood of Vancouver, free again. She wanted none of the past few days to have happened. Or, for that matter, the previous month. Outside, the light changed; dark gray clouds rolled in, and slowly, quietly, it began to rain.

Tristanne pulled out her mobile and called her mother, who was, after all, the reason she was standing in Florence in the first place instead of in her own living room, which she'd set up as a makeshift artist's studio and from where she had a view of nothing more remarkable than the backyard she shared with her neighbor. She loved that yard, Tristanne reminded herself as the phone rang. She liked to sit out in it with a glass of wine when the evenings were fine. She did not know why she felt as if she needed to defend it to herself now, much less the rest of her life—as if it was all slipping out of her reach with every breath.

"Oh, darling!" Vivienne cried into the phone when she answered. No sign in her voice of her illness, her persistent cough or her unexplained fevers. Tristanne wondered what it cost her—though she knew her mother would never complain. "Are you having a lovely holiday?"

Which was, Tristanne thought when she ended the call a few moments later, really the most she could expect from her mother. Her flighty, fragile, unendingly sweet mother, who had spent her life being looked after by one man or another. Her father, her husband, her stepson. She was anachronistic, Tristanne often thought, with varying degrees of frustration— a throwback to another time, a different world. And yet she had always been the single bright light in Tristanne's life—the only thing that had made her childhood bearable. Vivienne had been a flash of bright colors and boundless enthusiasm in the midst of so much grim, cold darkness. And now she was unwell, and needed her daughter. Tristanne would do anything for her. Anything at all.

Even this.

"You must take pictures," Vivienne had said, nearly bubbling over with her excitement—which was at least an improvement over her grief, or her weakness. "You must record your adventures for posterity!" Because a lady did not discuss the reasons for a trip like Tristanne's, just as a lady did not discuss her debts, or her failing health.

"I'm not sure this is the sort of trip I'll want to remember," Tristanne had said dryly, but her mother had only laughed gaily and changed the subject.

What pictures should she take to capture the moment? Tristanne wondered now, her mind reeling. She pressed a hand against her temple. What would best express the Nikos Katrakis experience? What single image would conjure up the dizzy madness of the last two days?

She did not—*would not*—think of his wicked mouth on hers, his hands smoothing fire and need into her skin until she'd shaken with it. She could not think of his devastating quiet on that darkened street, the way he had held her captive with only that dark, too-perceptive gaze. His cutting mockery, that beguiling almost-smile… She wanted none of those images in her mind. She had to remember why she was here—why she was doing this.

She let her head fall forward until it touched the cool glass of the great window, and sighed. It seemed to take over her whole body.

She would do what she must, but that did not mean she had to sit here like this apartment, empty and discarded until Nikos condescended to return and begin their little dance anew. A whole city waited just outside, brimming with art and history in the summer rain, the perfect balm for the heart she told herself did not ache within her chest, the tears she would not allow herself to cry; for the life she suddenly feared would never fit her again as well as it used to, as well as it should.

CHAPTER SEVEN

HE WAS waiting for her when she rounded the corner.

At first she thought he was some kind of hallucination—
the same one she had been having to some degree or another
all afternoon, to her great irritation. She'd seen the side of his
head in the crowded rooms of the Uffizi Gallery, startling her
as she gazed at Botticelli's famous painting of Venus rising
from the water, all lush curves and flowing hair. But it had
only been a dark-haired father bending to whisper to his
two wriggling children, not Nikos at all. She'd glimpsed his
unmistakable saunter from a distance on the Ponte Vecchio,
the ancient bridge crowded full of shops and arches and tourists that stretched across the Arno—but then she had blinked
and seen the figure approaching her was nothing so special
after all, just a local man crossing a bridge.

So Tristanne did not immediately react when she saw
him this time, expecting the figure lounging in the archway
that led into Nikos's old building to turn to vapor, fade into
shadow, or step forward and reveal himself to be an ordinary
resident of the city, simply going about his business in the
wet summer evening.

But as she drew closer, her footsteps echoing off the ancient cobblestones, the image before her only intensified.
The jet-black hair. The dark, tea-steeped eyes, swimming
with gold and fire. The dragon in him infused his very skin,

making him seem almost to glow with all the power he held
carefully leashed in that lean, muscled torso, so wide through
the shoulders and narrow at his hips. He leaned against the
stone wall, protected from the rain, his long arms crossed
and his gaze intent upon her as she approached.

"Where have you been?"

The question seemed to echo even louder than her shoes
against the stones, and her heart beat like a drum in her
chest. Tristanne told herself that it was simply a trick of the
fading light and the effect of the rain, as the old city settled
into evening all around her. This section, hidden in a series
of twisted age-old streets that seemed to double back and
forth on top of each other, was so very quiet in comparison to
the high traffic areas she'd walked earlier. He only sounded
dangerous and on edge because there were not seas of tourists
to dull the sound of his voice.

And even if he was on edge, for some no doubt inscrutable
reason he would not bother to share with her, why should
she act as if that cowed her? She did not understand why
this man made her forget herself so easily, but she could not
let it continue. It did not matter how she *felt*, she reminded
herself—a key point she had returned to again and again as
she wandered through centuries of art all afternoon—it only
mattered how she *acted*.

"My apologies," she said, curving her mouth into an ap-
proximation of meek smile. "I had so hoped to beat you here,
so that I might arrange myself on your sofa like a still-life
painting. *Prettily*, of course. As directed."

He only watched her as she closed the distance between
them and stepped under the archway with him. She knew she
was soaked through, but she could not bring herself to care
as she no doubt should. The rain was warm, and had seemed
to her like some kind of necessary cleansing as she'd walked
through Florence's famous piazzas. As if she had needed to
bathe in all the sights and centuries arrayed before her, and

if the price of that was her bedraggled appearance now, well, so be it.

"You look half-drowned," he said after a long moment. His eyes were too hot on hers, too unsettling. "What could possibly be so important that it lured you out in this weather without so much as an umbrella?"

"I cannot imagine," she said dryly, pushing her damp hair back from her face. "Surely there is nothing in the whole of the city of Florence that could possibly interest an artist."

"Art?" He pronounced the word as if it was an epithet in some foreign language he did not know. His head tilted to the side as he looked down at her, arrogant and imperious. "Are you certain it was *art* that drew you into the streets, Tristanne? And not something significantly more prosaic?"

"Perhaps a man of your stature does not notice art until you purchase it to grace your walls, or to appear as a coveted view outside your windows," Tristanne said tartly, before she could think better of it. "But there are people in the world— and I realize this may surprise you—who find art just as moving when it is displayed in a public square as when it is hidden away in private collections for the amusement of the very rich."

"You will have to forgive me if I cannot live up to your rarified expectations," Nikos said coolly, though his eyes narrowed. "There were not many opportunities for art appreciation classes in my childhood, in public or private. I was more concerned with living through the week. But do not let me keep you from feeling superior because you can tell the difference between medieval sculptors at a glance. I am sure that is but one among many useful skills you possess."

"You will not make me feel badly about something that has nothing to do with me!" Tristanne threw at him, her cheeks hot with sudden embarrassment and a sinking sensation in the pit of her stomach that she refused to acknowledge. "You loom here, *oozing* your power from every pore, *dripping* luxury items like yachts and cars and sprawling flats, and yet *I* am supposed to feel badly because of your past? When you have obviously overcome it in every conceivable way and now flaunt it across Europe?"

His dark eyes glittered, and his mouth pulled to one side. Tristanne knew beyond a shadow of a doubt that she did not want to hear whatever cutting thing he was about to say—that he would shred her without a second thought, just to assuage whatever mood this was that had him in its grip.

"I am not the one with expectations," she hissed, hoping to stave him off. "You are."

"You expect me to believe you wandered around looking at art in the rain?" he asked after a long, brooding moment. There was an urgency in his tone, a certain intensity, that she didn't understand. That she didn't *want* to understand, because she didn't *want* to feel the urge to comfort him, to soothe him, however unlikely it was that he might let her do such a thing. She wanted only to complete this task, to gain her trust fund. That was the only thing she could allow herself to want.

"I do not care if you believe it or not," she said instead, confused by the direction of her thoughts. She raised her shoulders only to let them fall again. "It is what I did."

"And why would you do this?" His dark gaze moved over her face, and she was afraid, suddenly, of the things he might see, the urges he might notice and use against her. She looked away, back toward the street, letting her gaze follow the shadows and graze the cobblestones. She crossed her arms over her chest, half to appear defiant, but half to hold herself still as well.

"I suppose you will tell me a mistress does not do such a thing," she said softly, shaking her head slightly at the water coursing down the street. "I imagine the perfect mistress…

what? Shops for outfits she does not need? Sits in a room and contemplates the state of her hair?"

He almost smiled. She could sense it more than see it, in the closeness of that archway, hidden away together from the falling rain and coming dark.

"Something like that," Nikos said. "She certainly does not roam the streets in a wild state, dripping wet and looking primitive."

She looked at him then, and something flashed between them, hot and intimate. Dangerous. Uncontrollable. Tristanne felt her breath catch, and released it, deliberately. *Count to ten*, she cautioned herself. *Do not fan this fire—it will burn you alive. It will ruin everything.*

"I only said I wanted to be your mistress," she said slowly, her voice lower and huskier than she'd intended, as if it had plans of its own. "I never said anything about being perfect."

Something about her undid him. Her wide brown eyes, perhaps, so clever and yet so wary. The tilt of that chin, so pugilistic, as if she wanted to fight him, hold him off, defy him at all costs when her very presence here as his supposed mistress should have ensured the opposite. That lush, wide mouth that he wanted to taste again, every time he looked at it. And the way that green dress clung, wet and heavy, to curves that he was beginning to believe might haunt him for the rest of his days.

It did not matter that he had deep suspicions about her activities this afternoon. Had she met with her pig of a brother? Had she received further orders, whatever those might be? He could not seem to get a hold of the searing anger he felt when he thought about such a meeting—and he had been unable to think of anything else since he'd arrived back at the flat to find her out, whereabouts unknown. He knew it made no sense. It was not logical, or rational. She had never pretended to owe him any allegiance, and he had known she must have ulterior motives the moment she'd walked up to him on his yacht. He knew why he was using her—why should he think she was not using him equally?

"No," he said slowly, pushing away from the wall. "We cannot call you perfect, certainly."

She blinked. "That sounds significantly more insulting when you say it."

He wanted to demand that she tell him what her game was, that she admit whatever nefarious scheme she'd cooked up with her vile brother. As if it would mean something, such a confession. As if it would somehow excuse the need for her that itched in him, that he was beginning to worry was not, as it ought to be, purely physical.

The urge to take her, to lose himself in her lush body, to drown in her sweet and spicy scent, in her soft skin, in her scalding heat—all of that was completely understandable. Expected, even. Part and parcel of his ultimate revenge. It was…this other thing that was driving him insane. The odd and novel urge to leave her untouched at the door to her stateroom the night before, with only a gruff demand that she meet him for breakfast. Why had he done that? That had not been the way he'd planned the night at all.

But he had lost his purpose, somehow, between the oddly quiet moment after her outburst on the streets of Portofino and the stunned, hurt look in her eyes after he had ripped into her about her *exalted standards*. If he was someone else, he might have wondered if he'd been loathe to hurt her feelings—which was impossible as well as ridiculous, for how did he expect to enact a fitting revenge on her family without doing exactly that? In spades? It was as if she bewitched him somehow, with her frowns and her challenges, her sharp tongue and her unexpected naps—all things that should have made him dismiss her entirely.

And would have, he told himself fiercely, if she was anyone else.

"And now you are scowling at me," Tristanne said, her eyes scanning his face as she frowned back at him. "I don't know what it is you think I did—"

"What haven't you done?" he asked, almost as an aside. Almost as if he asked himself, not her. Perhaps he did, though he had little hope of an answer.

"I haven't done anything at all!" she protested.

"That, too," he said, and sighed. And then gave up.

He reached over and hooked his hand around her crossed arms, tugging her toward him with very little effort. She came without a fight, her expressive face registering a series of emotions—confusion, worry, and what he wanted to see most of all. Desire.

He pulled her off balance, deliberately, so that she sprawled across the wall of his chest and he could feel, finally, her soft breasts pressed into him, her body sodden and warm against his. Her head tipped back so she could look at him, her brown eyes wide and grave but with that heat within.

"Nikos," she began, that slight frown appearing again between her brows.

He did not know what he meant to do until he did it. He leaned down and pressed his lips to that serious wrinkle, smoothing it away, hearing her gasp even as he felt it against the skin at his neck.

"I think—" she started again.

"You think too much," he muttered, and then he kissed her.

He wanted lust, fire, passion, and those things were there, underneath. She tasted of the rain, and something else. Something sweet. He could not seem to get enough of it. Of her. He cradled her face between his hands, and kissed her again and again, until they were both gasping for breath.

He pulled away, and, giving in to an urge he didn't

understand and didn't care to examine, tucked her beneath his chin. Her arms were folded still, her fists against his chest, and he held her there, listening to their hearts pound out their need together.

Mine, he thought, and knew he should thrust her away immediately. Put distance between himself and whatever spell this was, that made him feel things he could not allow himself to feel. It wasn't simply that he should only want her for a very specific reason—he knew better. Hadn't he paid this price already? Hadn't he vowed that he would never put himself in a position like this again? That he would not want what he could not have? He did not believe in the things that would make such moments as this possible. Redemption. Forgiveness. Those were for other men. Never for him. *He knew better.*

But he did not move.

"I don't understand you at all," she whispered. Her hands uncurled against him, and spread open, as if to hold him. As if she could heal him with her touch. As if she knew he was broken in the first place.

He did not believe in any of that, either. He knew exactly who she was and why she was here. What he must do, and would. Still, he did not push her away.

"Neither do I," he said.

And then stood there, holding her, much longer than he should.

Any leftover feelings Tristanne might have had from their interaction in the rain—and his devastatingly tender kisses— were obliterated the moment she saw herself in the dress.

"I brought you something to wear tonight," he had said when they entered the flat. His distance and cool tone should have alerted her, but did not. "I will leave it for you when you are finished with your shower."

"Tonight?" she had asked, her emotions still in a near-painful jumble. She'd told herself that was why his suddenly brusque tone seemed to rub her the wrong way, after those unexpected moments in the archway. Or perhaps it was just her impatience with herself, for being so emotional when she could so little afford it.

"It is a small business function," he had said with a dismissive shrug, and she had thought no more about it until it came time to pull the dress from the hanger where he had left it, suspended from the door inside the guest suite he had indicated she should use to get ready.

Now, her hair dried and blown out to hang in a straight, gleaming curtain, cosmetics carefully applied to accent and emphasize her eyes, she stared at herself in the full-length mirror that stood at an angle in the corner of the richly furnished room. But she could not see the royal blue and gold accents that graced the walls and brocaded the commanding, four-poster bed. She could hardly catch her breath. She could only stare at her reflection, literally struck dumb.

She felt herself flush, deep and red and panicked, so red she nearly matched the scarlet fabric that *barely* made up the dress she wore. He could not mean that he wanted her to wear what little there was of *this* dress, could he? She could not go out in public dressed like this! She could not leave the *room* dressed like this!

She tried to take a deep breath, and made a sound like a sob instead. She squeezed her eyes shut, and her hands into fists. Then, slowly, she opened her eyes and forced her hands to open, too.

The dress was obscene. There was no other word for it.

It clung to her body like paint, leaving nothing to the imagination. There was not a single curve that was not outlined by the tight, clinging garment that slicked its way from tiny capped sleeves to her midthighs. If she tried to cover a decent amount of her breasts, the hem rose to a scandalous height, and if she tugged the hem lower, she risked having her breasts fall out of the tiny bodice. There was no happy medium. It required that she remove her undergarments entirely, or risk calling more attention to them, so clearly outlined were they by the tight, too-tight, material.

There was only one kind of woman who wore a dress like this, Tristanne thought, humiliation thick in the back of her throat, and she was pretending to be one of them. Was this Nikos's goal? Did he *want* her to feel this way? Did he take pleasure in imagining Tristanne walking into a public event like this? So scandalously, tackily, *barely* attired?

Or, she thought, fighting back the angry tears that flooded her eyes, that she refused to shed, perhaps she was missing the point entirely. Perhaps he was not trying to embarrass her, necessarily—perhaps this was how he preferred to see his women dressed. Perhaps he liked to make his mistress's position perfectly clear to everyone he encountered. It need not be personal at all. It should not have felt like such a slap.

She glanced at the clock and saw that she had wasted far too much time, and was once again late. She bit at her lower lip as she looked at herself again, but she knew she had no choice but to brazen it out. She had to do what he wanted for just a little bit longer. Her mother had made it sound as if Peter was already in a much better frame of mind, which made Tristanne hopeful that her plan was working and this mad scheme of hers could end. Because she was not at all sure that she could take too much more of this…exposure, in all senses of the term.

But whatever might happen in the days to come, she still had to walk out of this room in this scandalous, appalling dress. She closed her eyes for a brief moment, a breath, and then turned on her heel and forced herself to leave the room before she could think better of it.

She found him in the living room, swirling whiskey in a crystal tumbler and staring out at the glorious Dome before him. He turned slowly, and Tristanne came to a stop in the center of the room to let him look his fill. Surely that was his intention—the point of this whole exercise?

"Is this what you had in mind?" she asked, her voice throatier than she would have liked, from all the emotions she was fighting to keep to herself, to keep inside. To pretend she did not feel at all.

His face was in shadow, yet she could still feel the searing heat of his dark gaze. She could feel it traveling over her exposed skin, making her nipples contract and goose bumps shiver across her shoulders. It was as if some unseen cord connected them, forcing her to react to him, however little she might wish to do so.

"Do I please you?" she asked, an edge in her voice that she could not control. "Is that not what mistresses ask?"

"If they do not, they should," he replied in that lethally quiet voice that made her knees weaken beneath her. She wanted to hate him. She did. "And I must congratulate you, Tristanne."

His mouth moved into that mocking curve, and she braced herself. But he moved closer, and there was no mistaking the hot, possessive gleam in his burnished dark gold eyes. Nor the answering throb that bloomed in her sex and made her mouth go dry.

What she would do to hate him! Or, at the very least, not to want him.

He reached over and took her hand, enveloping it in the heat of his own. Never taking his eyes from hers, pinning her to the spot and making her pulse flutter wildly in her temples, her throat, he raised her hand to his warm, full lips.

"You have finally met, if not exceeded, all my expectations," he murmured.

But what she heard was the sound of her own doom, the clang of a cage door slamming shut, as something in her she did not want to acknowledge whispered words she could not bring herself to accept. And it had nothing to do with her mother, with her reasons for being here. *You will never escape this man*, the voice told her, wise and deep, as something like truth twisted in her gut. *You will never be free of him.*

CHAPTER EIGHT

THE party Nikos took her to was neither small nor a stuffy business affair—it was a star-studded gala event held at the Palazzo Pitti, a vast Renaissance palace that had once been home to the Medicis, not far from the Ponte Vecchio on the south side of the Arno. The building was a cold and severe stone edifice that hovered imposingly over her, Tristanne thought, glancing up at the forbidding facade as Nikos helped her out of his car into the sudden blaze of flashbulbs.

Though in truth, the same could be said of Nikos.

Tristanne had no choice but to walk at his side as if she did not notice the second-looks, the ripple of whispers in her wake. She had no choice but to smile for the photographers who formed a scrum at the entrance to the palace, and pretend she was delighted to be seen out with Nikos, thrilled to be displayed like the spoils of war in a bimbo's dress. There was nothing she could do except attempt to handle the whole thing gracefully. She kept her head held high, her smile in place, and hoped that all the years of pretending to be made of Barbery ice would pay off now, when needed.

And after all, she reminded herself, the publicity was the point—not what she happened to be wearing.

Nikos led her into a courtyard open beneath the clear night sky. The rain had finally ended and the evening was warm and close, making the lights seem denser and more intriguing as they shone on the fountain up above and the white marble statues that stood frozen still in their giant stone alcoves. Aristocrats and matinee idols wore the finest Italian couture and dripped priceless gems, murmuring to each other over cocktails at small white-topped tables.

"What business is this, exactly?" Tristanne asked, glancing around. To her left she saw businessmen whose names were always mentioned in awed tones in newspaper editorials, to her right, a philanthropic rock star stood in deep conversation with a British socialite.

Nikos slanted a look down at her. "Mine," he said, with a certain amused finality.

"Meaning you own it?" Tristanne asked with asperity. "Or that you would like me to mind my own? A man in possession of as many things as you are really must be more clear."

Their eyes met, and once again, she felt a melting that shook her to her bones. Could it not leave her for even a moment? she wondered, in something like despair. Not even for tonight, when he had deliberately dressed her like a tart and dragged her here to make certain she—and half of Europe—knew her place? But none of that seemed to matter. He looked at her as if he knew things about her that she did not, yet, and she felt her chest constrict, her pulse race in helpless reaction, as if there was no greater purpose to her being with him than that. As if she was his mistress.

"Would you like a drink, Tristanne?" he asked softly.

"That would be lovely," she managed to say. "Thank you."

She watched him cut through the crowd on his way to the bar, his lean form expertly displayed in a dark Italian suit that made love to his wide shoulders and long legs. As he had on the yacht—had that been only days ago?—Nikos stood out from the rest. It was the simmering energy that he exuded as some men did cologne. It was the way he moved, restless and aware, ready for anything. His history showed in his body, she thought, if nowhere else. He was ready to fight, and his well-honed physique was his first weapon. It was why some avoided him, why others were drawn to him. He was a man, in the most traditional, physical sense of the term. She had no doubt that he knew what every single one of his muscles was for, and how best to use each one to get the better of an opponent. It was almost unfair that such a formidable physical presence was not the sum total of who he was—that it should merely be the packaging for a mind such as his, incisive and quick. He was like no one she had ever met. It was one more thing about him she wished she did not admire.

Not that it mattered, she reminded herself forcefully. She could admire him all she liked—it did not change what she must do, did it? She had known when she'd first approached him that this would be a terrible mistake. It had not stopped her then. And now it was much too late.

"Ah, Tristanne."

The sneering, hateful voice announced his identity, making her stiffen in surprise and dismay, before she turned to confirm it. *Peter.*

"I see you have finally embraced your true heritage," he continued.

She turned to face him fully, taking her time as if that might lessen her shock. Her brother stood before her, his dark eyes alive with malevolence. Could no one else see it? she wondered—and not for the first time. A well-cut suit could not hide the darkness in him, the bully he truly was. She had always seen it. She suspected he'd wanted her to see it, to fear it, from the start.

"Peter," she said with a great and abiding calm she did not feel. She forced herself not to look down at her arm, where the bruises he'd left were almost completely faded now—only a smudge or two of yellow remained as testament to his violence, his utter disregard for her. "What a delightful surprise."

"I asked myself what sort of trollop would parade through the Palazzo Pitti dressed like a two-dollar whore," he said in his most snide voice, just loud enough to insinuate itself into Tristanne's ear and make her feel dirty by association. "I should have known at once that it was you."

"Do you not like my dress?" she asked. She raised her brows, allowing herself no other expression, no outward sign of how her stomach heaved, how her pulse raced in panic. "Of course, Nikos picked it out. Would you prefer I fight with him over something so small as a dress?"

Peter only glared at her for a moment, his gaze cold. Tristanne ordered herself to gaze back with every appearance of unruffled tranquility.

"You have outdone yourself, my dear sister," he said after an uncomfortable moment, his lips curled. "I assumed Katrakis would use what you so blatantly offered him and cast you aside." His gaze raked over her, and she knew, with a scorching sense of shame, exactly what he could see, and in what detail. It made her wish she could disappear into the stones beneath her feet. Instead she stood straighter. "And yet here you are with him, tarted up at his command. How enterprising and inventive you have turned out to be."

She should feel triumphant, she realized as she looked at her brother. He believed she was Nikos's mistress. Her plan was working, just as she'd anticipated. So why did she feel so hollow instead?

"I want my trust fund," she told him flatly. She smiled then. "Wasn't this what you wanted? Surely Nikos Katrakis is *visible* enough to suit you? I believe our picture was taken at least fifty times as we walked in."

That had been his claim the night before she had boarded Nikos's boat—that her liaison must be with someone *visible*. He had wanted to choose the man, of course, for reasons

Tristanne would prefer not to investigate too closely. It was clear, he had shouted that awful night, that she would only make a fool of herself with a man like Nikos and then be ruined for his purposes. She'd suspected he'd simply wanted an excuse to put his hand on her and shake her. Hard. And so he had.

"Careful you do not overplay your hand," Peter retorted now, his eyes cold. "What is his angle? Have you figured it out?" When she did not respond, he laughed in a way that made her skin crawl. "Surely you don't believe that a man like Katrakis would find *you* quite so captivating, Tristanne. Perhaps he wishes to trade on the Barbery name himself." He shook his head, his lips thinning. "A man can climb out of the sewer, one supposes, but he still walks around with the stench of it."

Tristanne wanted to haul off and slap him for that, but she did not dare. *Think of your mother!* she warned herself. There was too much at stake. And Nikos did not need her to defend him to Peter, of all people. So why did she want to? She was not even sure where the urge to defend him had come from, nor why it lingered, making her stomach tense.

"He has not shared his ulterior motives with me," she said icily. "Just as I have neglected to share yours with him."

"You will need to keep him happy for the next few weeks, at least," Peter said offhandedly, his attention on the crowd around them, as if he was searching for more important people. "Perhaps a month."

"A month?" Tristanne clamped down on her panic, her anger. "Don't be absurd, Peter. That is far too long. The pictures taken tonight should be all you need."

"I will decide what I need, Tristanne, thank you," he snapped. His gaze narrowed, and an insinuating smile played on his thin lips. "What's the matter? Afraid you don't have what it takes to keep Katrakis's interest? I have heard his tastes are…earthy."

"I want my trust find," she said again, more succinctly. She did not know what Peter meant by that comment, nor wish to know. Though her imagination could not help but supply vivid images to suit the word earthy, each more devastating than the last. Nikos's hot, tender mouth upon her flesh, his strong, capable hands lifting her, his whipcord strength all around her, above her—

"It will take a month," Peter said, snapping Tristanne back into the courtyard with a jolt. Peter's cold eyes bored into her. "But if it makes you feel any better, I think it is clear that you have found your life's work." He laughed, unpleasantly.

He thinks I am nothing but a whore, Tristanne thought dully. Yet she could not seem to summon up any outrage on her own behalf. After all, he always had. The only difference was that now, if she peeled away the shocking heat that consumed her whenever she thought of Nikos, she feared that Peter might be right. And worse, that she might like it where Nikos was concerned—but she could not allow herself such incendiary thoughts!

"I want to see the paperwork regarding the transfer of my funds by next week." She gazed at him coldly, determined to look unafraid. Unaffected. "Is that clear enough? Do we understand each other?"

"I understand you better than you think, *sister,*" Peter hissed at her, the word *sister* sounding like a vicious insult, like the hard slap he no doubt wished to give her. But Tristanne did not recoil. Not even when he smiled that horrible smile. "All the years you spent spouting off about your *principles* and your *honor,* and all the while you were no better than a whore, just waiting for the right price." He waited, letting that sink in, and then his nasty smile deepened. "Exactly like your mother."

Each word, she knew, was carefully calculated to maim, to wound. To prey on her feelings for Vivienne and force her to reveal herself. But she would rather die than give him the satisfaction of knowing he'd been successful. She would keep what she felt locked down, hidden away. She would not react. *She would not.*

"Next week, Peter," she said through her teeth. "Or you can forget the whole thing."

His eyes narrowed, that malevolent gleam flaring to sickening life, and she braced herself for whatever he might say next.

But instead she felt her body thrill to a sudden heat beside her, and knew without looking that Nikos had returned. Was it absurd that she felt as if he'd saved her, simply by standing beside her? *It is certainly foolish,* she admonished herself. Nonetheless, relief—thick and sweet—flooded through her. She had the insane urge to move closer to him, to burrow against his hard chest as if they were truly lovers, as if he would care for her in that way, protect her, but she shook it off.

"Katrakis." Peter nodded in greeting, looking at Nikos with ill-concealed distaste.

Nikos smiled. It was that wolf's smile, far too dangerous, and Tristanne knew that Peter was out of his depth even if he seemed to be unaware of that fact. She took a deep breath, feeling her spine ease its erect posture just a bit.

"Barbery," Nikos said, his arrogant brows raised and his expression faintly amused. Tristanne could see how little Peter liked it. His gaze darkened.

"When my sister announced that she was spending a few days sailing to Greece, I could not imagine she meant with you," Peter said.

As if there was some other Nikos Katrakis? What game was he playing now? Not for the first time, Tristanne wondered *why* Peter hated Nikos so much, when surely Nikos was exactly the sort of man Peter normally attempted to cultivate. All she had ever known was that Peter hated even the mention of his name, and always had.

"What, I wondered, could a Katrakis want with a Barbery?" Peter asked.

"It cannot be a mystery to you, surely," Nikos drawled. Tristanne felt her skin prickle with heat. Nikos's smile deepened, turned more mocking. "Buy me a drink sometime and I will clear it up for you."

"My sister is usually not quite so charming as you seem to find her," Peter said darkly, as if he was discussing a fractious mare or a disobedient hound. "I am amazed you have found her so…congenial."

"No doubt your amazement is what caused you to lose your head and put your hands upon her," Nikos said then, his voice smooth and deadly, like a whip. His eyes flashed dark gold fire. To Tristanne's shock—and shame—he reached over and sketched the back of his fingers across the fading bruises on her upper arm, though he never looked away from Peter. "For surely you must know that I prefer that what is mine bear no mark but my own."

She did not care for that, Nikos could tell. He was learning to read her now, and though her facial expression remained remote, almost bored, he could feel her tense beneath his hand. She did not look up at him, though that defiant chin inched upward. She kept her eyes trained on the snake before her, her brother, who could not keep the vicious glee from his own gaze.

Nikos had expected Peter's presence—it was why they had come to Florence in the first place—but he had not anticipated the hard kick of anger that had spiked through his gut when he'd seen the vicious look on Peter's face, and Tristanne's carefully blank expression. It had taken him by surprise. He told himself it was because Barbery believed that he'd won, that he'd planted Tristanne with Nikos and Nikos was none the wiser. He told himself that it had nothing to do with his protective urges toward this woman, urges he could not permit himself to indulge unless they aided him in his revenge against the swine of a man before him.

"But you have spent time with her now," Peter said, with a shrug. "I do not need to tell you how difficult it is to keep her in line, do I?"

Nikos wanted to destroy Peter. He told himself that was the way he would feel no matter what the man had said, simply because of who he was, but he knew better. He knew exactly why he wanted to wrap his hands around Peter Barbery's throat.

It made an alarm sound deep within him. But, defying all logic, he ignored it.

"I do not find it difficult at all," he said quietly.

"Then you must have abilities that I do not," Peter said, in a sneering voice that Nikos did not much care for. "I confess that our father found her so tiresome that he washed his hands of her years ago."

"I am, in fact, standing right here," Tristanne said crisply, her brown eyes snapping with temper—and something far darker. "I can hear you."

Peter smirked, but continued to gaze at Nikos. "Or perhaps your definition of *keeping her in line* and mine differ," he said with a sniff. "She is too insolent by half. A trait she gets, no doubt, from her mother."

"My mother is many things," Tristanne said with marked calm. Nikos admired her smile, so pointed and bright, and her seeming ease. He believed neither. "But insolent is not one of them. Come now, Peter. Must we air our family laundry in public? I am certain Nikos must be bored to tears."

"And by all means," Peter said in that oily voice, "you must keep Katrakis happy."

Nikos felt her tense again next to him, as if she was contemplating hurling herself at her brother and pummeling him into a pulp with her fists. Or perhaps that was only his own desire, projected upon her. Either way, the conversation had served its purpose. Nikos wanted to waste no more time on Peter Barbery than strictly necessary.

"You will excuse us," he said abruptly to Peter, dismissing him with an offhanded arrogance he knew would enrage the other man. "I must circulate."

"Of course," Peter said, with an icy nod. He turned his gaze on his sister. She smiled at him, if something that frigid could pass for a smile. And then Peter moved off into the crowd without a backward glance.

Giving into an urge he could not name, and did not want to admit, Nikos slid his arm around her bare shoulders, pulling her closer to the expanse of his chest.

Tristanne looked up at him then, her eyes dark and stormy. He could not sort through the emotion he saw there. But he could see that same fire banked in her that he knew was in him, even now. She was too responsive. Too aware of his every move. How was he to resist that? Why was he bothering to try?

This is all part of your revenge, he reminded himself. *Even this. Especially this.* But he was not certain, suddenly, if he believed it.

Nikos handed her the drink he had procured for her, having foregone his own when he'd seen her brother approach her, and noted that her hand was trembling slightly as she took the wineglass from him. It was the only outward sign he could see that her brother had affected her.

"You and your brother do not get along," he observed in a low voice. It was an absurd understatement, and her mouth curved into something near a smile.

"In our family, emotions were viewed as the enemy," she said. "Woe betide the person who showed them, no matter the circumstances. We were expected to be perfect little automatons, smiling on command, and attending to my father's wishes without so much as an altered expression." She shrugged, and stepped away, out from under his arm. He let her go, reluctantly. "So you see, I am not certain Peter gets along with anyone. But he would never show it either way." She did not look at him, and Nikos could not understand why he wanted her to. Badly. She took a careful sip from her glass instead.

Nikos could not make sense of his own urges. Everything was proceeding exactly as he'd planned it, aside from today's strange interlude in the rain. He was squiring the Barbery heiress in front of cameras, at an event filled with business associates and gossipmongers. To say nothing of her despicable brother. The fact that they were an item would be assumed—and there would be few who would not speculate about any relationship between Nikos Katrakis and a Barbery. Nikos was not the only one with a long memory. When it came time to spurn her as Althea had been spurned years ago, it would be all the more devastating, all the more embarrassingly public. He was sure of it. It was just as he wanted it.

But all he could really concentrate on was that damned dress.

It licked over her curves, plastered itself to them and dared any man in the vicinity to notice another woman in all of Florence. Nikos could not tear his eyes away from her. She stood out like a ripe, hot flame, begging to be touched. She did not look trashy, as he had intended, thinking it some kind of punishment for her obstinacy. In truth, he had expected her to refuse to wear the dress at all.

But instead, she had beaten him at his own game. The dress was pure sex, a wicked invitation to her lush, tight body. And yet she looked almost aristocratic, as if the tight dress were the perfect accessory for her beauty, her position. It was the serene smile she wore, as if she had never been more comfortable in her life that she was in that scant dress, standing on the arm of a man who made no attempt to hide the fact that he would much prefer to be deep inside her than attending this function. Surely everyone could see his desires, written across his face. He hardly cared.

He could not remember ever wanting another woman more.

"You are staring at me," she said after a long moment. The tension spun out between them, shimmering and unmistakable, and Nikos knew that he was finished waiting. He had to have her, and to hell with his reasons *why*. It felt as if it had been years. Decades. A lifetime.

"You are mesmerizing," he said, his voice low. "But surely you know it."

"You are the one who found this dress," she said. Finally she looked at him. Her eyes were melted chocolate, rich and dark, a temptation he could no longer resist. "I am merely wearing it."

"It is the way you wear it," he told her, standing too close, not daring to touch her as every cell in his body demanded. Not here. Not in public. Not where he would have to stop. "I want to take it off you. With my teeth."

CHAPTER NINE

THE ride back to the flat passed in a liquid kind of silence, heavy and weighted, yet shimmering with unmistakable heat.

She had not agreed to anything, Tristanne reminded herself. She had only gazed at him and that addicting fire in his dark eyes, and he had not said another word. He had led her from the courtyard, fetched the car from the valet and handed her into it with a quiet chivalry completely at odds with the frank sensual hunger in his gaze.

Before she knew it they were back in that vast loft of a living room high above the ancient streets. She was caught between the epic grandeur of the Duomo on the other side of the window behind her and the heavy front door to the flat that Nikos shut tight and bolted, locking them in.

Locking *her* in.

Suddenly the enormous space seemed to contract, until there was nothing but that hot, hard gleam in his dark eyes. Tristanne felt her heart beat, wild and loud, in her throat, her temples, her chest, her sex. She wanted to run, then—run through the old streets and over the cobblestones, run and run and run as if that might make this feeling disappear, as if she could leave it behind somehow. That same thought that had troubled her earlier in the evening returned, with force. She could not escape him. She would never be free of him.

But not, she thought now with devastating insight, because he would chase her—but because for all her panic and her pounding heart, she did not move. Could not move. Did not *want* to move.

Dragon, she thought almost helplessly, and she knew with a deep certainty that she was about to see his real fire—the flames she had been dancing around since the moment she'd met him. The powerful conflagration that had always been there, waiting in his dark gaze, his mocking smile, while she'd tried to talk her way out of exactly this moment. The fire that she knew would consume her, immolate her, turn her into nothing more than ash.

Still, she did not turn away from him. She did not scream, or run for her room, or for the streets, or do anything except hold his gaze. She did not understand how she could be so fascinated with him even when she knew he was the reason for her panic. She did not know how now, when it mattered the most, she could be so heedless of her own self-preservation. He stood opposite her, that half smile carved into the sculpted leanness of his hard jaw, his dark eyes making the kind of sensual promises that made her feel shaky, intoxicated.

"Come here," he said, his voice a ribbon of sound across the elegant room, seductive and stirring. Tristanne felt it against her skin like a caress. Like another one of his promises, the ones her body ached for—the ones she knew she had to fight off at all costs.

"I don't think so," she said. She hadn't meant to say it—had she? She only knew that she could not let this happen. She could not surrender to this man. *She could not.* And not only because of her ulterior motives. She coughed slightly. "I think, in fact, that I will stay over here instead."

His smile deepened, turned dangerous in ways that made her nipples peak and her belly tauten, further signs that she was in so far over her head, she might as well consider herself half-drowned.

"Of course not." But he did not seem angry, or even particularly tense. Instead his gaze moved over her, sending heat flashing across every place on her overtly displayed body that his eyes touched. When his eyes met hers again, he seemed almost relaxed. Almost. "Why am I not surprised?"

"You promised…" she began, but she lost track of the sentence because he moved, that long, rangy body eating up the distance between them with sure strides. He shrugged out of his jacket and tossed it aside, in the general direction of the grand sofa that commanded one wall. Never taking his eyes from hers, he removed his cuff links in a few quick jerks and dropped them on the wide, wooden coffee table.

He stalked toward her, and she knew he was doing it deliberately. Openly. She could not seem to summon breath to fill her lungs, much less the will to step back, to avoid him.

"No," he said, as he came to a stop a scant few inches in front of her. His voice was soft, his gaze so hot, so terribly, impossibly hot, and she felt an echo of that dangerous fire flash through her. "No, I did not promise you a thing, Tristanne."

"Of course you did," she contradicted him desperately, that thrumming, tightening panic making her scowl at him. "And even if you did not, what does it matter? Surely the great Nikos Katrakis does not have to take unwilling women to his bed!"

"Do you see such a creature in this flat?" he asked, his eyes molten gold and impossible to look away from. "Perhaps you see unicorns, too?"

"You cannot imagine that anyone could turn you down, can you?" she threw at him, her head spinning, her chest tight, as if she had in fact been running all this time, putting all of Florence between her and this man.

Instead of what she was actually doing, which was simply standing there, hoping her legs would hold her up, hoping the bravado that had gotten her through every other complicated interaction with this man would keep her going just a little bit longer. Just this one night more.

He smiled then, a real smile, for all that it was stamped with a deeply male satisfaction that seared through her, making her eyes heat and her sex pulse in want, in need. In that instinctive, insane response to him that she could not seem to control, nor reason away.

"I cannot imagine that *you* can turn me down, Tristanne," he said quietly, that undercurrent of certainty, of command, somehow more shattering than anything he might have said. "But by all means, prove me wrong."

He began to unbutton his shirt as he stood there, looking down at her like some kind of ancient god, all arrogant male confidence and power. Tristanne swallowed convulsively as her eyes, of their own accord, dropped to follow the widening swathe of smooth, olive-toned skin, brushed with a dusting of jet-black hair.

She could not remember her arguments, her strategies. It was as if the entire world had disappeared—all she was, all she had been, all she had planned to do—and all she wanted was to touch the hard male flesh he was unveiling so close in front of her. Taunting her, she was sure. Torturing her.

"I don't know what you're doing," she managed to say, somehow. "This display is highly unlikely to make me change my mind. I told you on the boat—"

"We are not on the boat," he said, amusement and fierce, unmistakable intent in his gaze, in his voice.

He peeled his shirt back from the hard planes of his chest and let it drop from his arms, and then there was no more hiding from his stark male beauty, rough and compelling, hard-worn steel covered in satin. He was the most glorious man she had ever seen, and she was trembling with the effort it took to keep her hands away from the expanse of smooth, muscled *male* that stood so tantalizingly close. *So close.* She curled her hands into tight balls, her fingernails digging into the soft flesh of her palms.

"Nikos…" she whispered, and she knew then that she was lost. All she had was her bravado, her reckless, hopeless willingness to fight the inevitable against all odds. To throw words at him in desperation, because she had nothing else. And if she could not deflect him, if she could not keep him at arm's length…

"I told you," he said in that velvet and whiskey voice that thrilled her deep in her feminine core, in ways she did not dare admit to herself. "You need only tell me that you have reached your limits. You need only say the word."

There was a moment then, shimmering and tense, when she wavered. When she thought in a brief burst of something darker than mere bluster that she could do it, that she could say the one small word that would end this. As she should. As she knew she should. She opened her mouth to say what she knew she ought to say, what she knew she must say if she was to survive this encounter with this tempting, impossible man.

"Nikos…" she breathed.

The fire in his dark gold eyes flared to a blaze, and his mouth moved into a hard, triumphant curve.

"That is not the word," he said, satisfaction coloring his low, knowing tone.

But she still did not, could not, say it.

He reached over, and traced the shape of her cheek with one large, confident hand. His palm was too hot, his fingers too clever. Her skin was too sensitive, too raw. But, unaccountably, she felt herself sway toward his hand, not away from it.

"Tell me to stop," he urged her, his eyes nearly black now with a passion she could not help but feel, humming through her like electricity, making her yearn for things she knew on some deep, primitive level would destroy her.

Giving in to an urge that was so intense it nearly felt like pain, Tristanne reached over and placed her palms against the wall of his chest. Heat exploded through her hands and ricocheted up her arms, searing a path that led directly to her swollen breasts, her aching sex. He hissed in a breath, then let it out in a sound that was too harsh to be a laugh.

"Tell me to stop," he said again, a taunt, and then he pulled her toward him and fitted his mouth to hers.

The dark sorcery of his mouth, his taste, overwhelmed her. Tristanne forgot everything. He kissed her like they would both perish if he stopped, and she kissed him back as if she believed him. She tasted the warm, tanned skin of his strong neck, let her hands trace the magnificent male architecture of his ridged abdomen, so much heat and power, all of it like warm, hard rock beneath her hands.

His hands dove into her hair, anchoring her head in place so he could tease her lips with his, tasting her again and again, pausing only to whisper words in Greek she could not understand, hot and dark words that inflamed her, made her try to move closer to him, to press against his wicked body with her own.

She felt the room tilt and whirl around her, and realized only as her back met the softest suede, that he had picked her up and laid her down on the sofa. He stretched out above her.

Finally, she thought, as his body came up hard against hers. It was too much and it was not enough, and she could not stop touching him.

"Tell me," he said roughly, as his hard chest crushed her breasts with a delicious pressure, as her hips cradled his maleness, hard and hot, as she gasped in delight and a kind of sensual terror. "Tell me, Tristanne."

Some part of her objected, in some dim corner of her mind—how could he still have the presence of mind to taunt her when she was very nearly in pieces? And yet the same deep, feminine part of her that had warned her away from this man knew, now, that her power lay not in words, but in an age-old knowledge that seemed to flood into her as she stared up at his face, so dark and determined above her.

She did not speak. She merely moved her hips in a lazy circle, and had the instant satisfaction of making him groan and grow, if possible, harder against her. He muttered something incoherent, and took her mouth again, his own insistent, demanding.

She met his demands, gloried in them. His hands slicked down the sides of that scandalous dress, tracing the curves he had displayed so unapologetically for all of Florence to see. He moved from her mouth, tracing a searing path down to her breasts, tasting them through the material. Hot, wet heat. Tristanne arched against the delicate torture of his mouth, gasping, as a tremor snaked through her, lighting her up from her sex to the tips of her toes.

His dark eyes caught hers, then, as he reached between them, his movements sure, his gaze like some kind of heat lightning. He pulled the stretchy fabric up around her waist, and then released his own trousers. As if they had done this a thousand times before, as if she knew his moves as well as her own, she wrapped her legs around his hips.

Tristanne felt that mad fever break over her, making her flush with want, with heat, with hunger. She moved against him mindlessly, helplessly. He angled his hips, held her thigh in his strong, commanding grasp, and in one, sure stroke, sheathed himself deep inside her.

She might have screamed. She thought she did—she could hear the echo of it, the force of it, ricocheting through her, the pleasure almost too much, almost too great to bear.

"Tell me to stop, Tristanne." It was a hoarse whisper. A taunt, or perhaps a dare. She was too far gone to care which.

"Stop!" she threw at him, fiercely, surprising them both.

He froze at once. *"Talking,"* she hissed. Her hands fisted against his broad, hard back. "Stop talking!"

A breathless, impossible moment. His hard length so deep inside of her she could not tell where she ended and he began, the pleasure emanating in waves from every place their bodies touched, the dress plastered to her, trapping her—and his dark, addictive gaze, seeing so far inside of her she knew she should be afraid of what he would know.

But instead, he moved.

She fit him like a glove. Like a benediction.

She was wrapped around him, her spicy-sweet scent and her soft moans almost too much for him to bear. Almost. He pulled himself back from the edge with iron control, and angled himself back so he could look down at her.

She was wild with passion beneath him, her eyes dark with need, her lips parted. Her hair was tangled from his fingers, her mouth slightly reddened from his kisses. A rosy glow brightened her skin, made her look even warmer, even hotter, than she felt against him. The scarlet dress wrapped around her lushness like a candy wrapper. She looked edible. Her hips moved beneath his, demanding and hungry, as if she could not get enough of him.

Mine, he thought again, from a dark place inside of him he did not care to explore, yet still rang through him with the force of a vow. He ignored it, and concentrated instead on those tiny noises she made in the back of her throat. On her long, shapely calves that were pressed against his hips, urging him on, deeper, closer.

He thrust into her slowly, deliberately, setting a lazy, unhurried pace that soon had her panting in a mixture of need and frustration. Her hips rose to meet his. Her back arched as she fought to get closer, to speed him on. He ignored his own hunger, her wordless demands, even the pounding of his own blood, and kept it slow. Easy.

Devastating.

He felt the fire build in her, the tremors that began to make her quiver. Her eyes fluttered shut, and her breath came faster and faster, as her moans turned to helpless pleading. Still, he waited, maintaining that same measured pace, that same iron mastery, turning her incandescent beneath him.

She was so alive. So vivid. *His*.

When her head began to toss against the cushions, he bent to the tempting swells of her breasts, and began to lick the sweet flesh he found there, spilling out from her bodice. She tasted like cream with the faintest hint of peach, and her own feminine musk. She went straight to his head like the finest whiskey, making him surge against her like an untried boy. He peeled back the bodice of the dress and let her plump, round breast free. Then, never breaking his rhythm, he began to learn each breasts with his lips, his tongue, the faintest hint of his teeth.

She cried out his name, a broken sound of uninhibited passion. Of mindless pleasure. And that was when he found her nipple, sucking the peak into his mouth with a gentle insistence.

This time, she screamed his name. And when she hurtled over the edge, he followed.

CHAPTER TEN

THERE were things he should think about, he knew; strategies he should put into place and advantages he should press, even while his heart thudded out a jagged beat. There would never be a better time to start the slow and steady process of destroying her family. Her. But she lay there beneath him so soft and warm, her eyes closed and her breath still coming hard, and Nikos could think of none of those things.

He was still inside of her, and he wanted her again. Immediately. He could not make sense of it. Hunger moved through him, making up his mind for him. There would be time enough to think, to plot. Now was the time to slake his unshakeable thirst for this most maddening, most inconvenient of women.

He moved, pulling himself away, and was pleased to see her stir as if reluctant to let him go. Her brown eyes opened, wary and still dazed with passion. She blinked at him as if she was not sure whether or not she had dreamed him. He stood up, kicking off his trousers. Her eyes darkened, and she propped herself up on her elbows, watching him carefully. Cautiously.

Did she know the wanton, disheveled picture she made? She sprawled across the sofa, a scarlet band of bunched-up dress clinging to her waist, her breasts free and her long legs splayed before her. He should, he knew, point out that she looked more like a mistress ought to in this moment than ever before. Compliant. Alluring. Thoroughly debauched. He knew saying such things would put them back on to the solid ground he had the strangest feeling he had lost somewhere while losing himself in the delirium of her body.

But he did not say a word, and he could not have told himself why not.

Instead he reached down and picked her up as if she weighed nothing, as if she were insubstantial. She gasped as he lifted her, holding her high against his chest, but she did not speak. Instead she let her head drop onto his shoulder, her hair falling to cover her—almost as if she was hiding.

He should call her on that weakness. He should force her to face him. He should make sure they both had nowhere to hide. Because hiding places suggested intimacy, and that was impossible. This was sex. Long overdue sex, that was all.

That had to be all.

He set her down on her feet in the lushly appointed bath that sprawled next to his master suite. He did not meet her gaze, though he could feel her looking at him, searching his expression. He preferred to look at her body, he told himself. It was a work of art. Skin of cream and pink and gold, up-turned breasts, and that band of tight scarlet wrapped around her middle, emphasizing the perfection of her figure, the swell of her hips and her long, silken legs.

Silently he reached down and took hold of the red dress, tugging it up and over her breasts and then helping her move the heavy mass of her hair through it. He cast it aside, and only then did he look at her.

She moistened her lower lip with her delicate tongue, making a new hunger uncoil within him. He leaned down and tasted the shape of her lips, that full, sweet bow, and then tested that delicate tongue with his own. He meant only to maintain this quiet between them, as if it was a sacred thing, though he refused to think of it that way—but her taste went to his head again, making him hard and ready. Unwilling to wait. Unable to think. As desperate to have her as if he had not just done so.

He pulled her flush against him, pressing his maleness against the soft skin of her belly. She gasped, and then shivered, bracing her small hands on his chest. He saw the tiny goose bumps rise along the curve of her arms.

"Nikos," she began, in a shaky kind of whisper.

"Hush," he murmured. He kissed her neck, and ran his hands along the seductive line of her spine, following it to the breathtaking swell of her hips. He tested the weight of her pert, round bottom in his hands, and then slipped his fingers lower, curving around into her furrow, finding her soft and hot.

Just as ready for him as he was for her. A flash of possessiveness roared through him.

"Do not tell me—" she started, in that same breathy voice, and he could not allow it. If she started playing her little games again, he would have to think about the many reasons he should be handling this moment differently, and then he would have to do so.

"Hush," he said again, and he took her hips between his hands and lifted her high into the air, sliding her breasts against the wall of his chest.

She gasped again, but threw her arms around him, clutching fast to his shoulders. He slid his hands down to her delectable behind and then, propping her up with his hands and holding her in place, he thrust into her, hard. She stiffened, then let out a long, low moan and let her head fall forward against the crook of his neck. He could feel her mouth there, open against his skin, her sudden, labored breathing electrifying his own, making his heart beat faster, harder.

"Put your legs around my waist," he ordered her, widening his stance. She obeyed him at once, locking her ankles in the small of his back. It was as if she had been made for him, carefully engineered for this slick, impossibly perfect fit. He lifted her slowly, then let her sink back down, making them both shudder as his hard length filled her completely.

He did it again. Then again. Then one more long, slow stroke of her body against his, his shaft deep inside her, and she began to shake against him, sobbing out her pleasure against his neck. He waited for her to stop shaking, still hard within her, and then sank down to his knees into the thick, soft carpet beneath their feet. Never releasing her from that most intimate contact between them, he settled her on to her back beneath him, nestling himself between her soft thighs.

She was still breathing heavily, and her chocolate eyes were dazed when she finally opened them. It took her a long moment to focus on him.

When she did, he smiled. He could not seem to help himself. But he could not bring himself to worry about that as he knew he should.

"My turn," he said.

She was lost.

Tristanne clung to Nikos's sinfully hard body, and, impossibly, felt herself start to quicken once again with every long, slow stroke. He loomed over her, his dark gold eyes serious, his face drawn with passion.

It should not be like this. She should not have been capable of the feelings he invoked in her. She should not have felt as if his slightest touch might send her spinning into ecstasy. Or at the very least, she should fight it. But with every thrust of his powerful body, she found she could not think of anything save him, as if nothing existed except the two of them and the sensations that threatened to overcome her entirely.

Too soon, too quickly, she felt her breath catch. It should not have been possible. It should not have felt more electric, more overwhelming, with every slick movement of his hips.

He murmured encouragement in dark, rich words she could not understand, pressing his mouth against her neck, and into her hair.

He reached between them, and pressed against her hidden nub, making her writhe against him and then, at his soft command, explode into pieces. She heard his hoarse shout, and then, for a time, knew nothing.

He did not let her rest too long. Instead he pulled her into the wide, luxurious expanse of his shower. Multiple jets of water created steam and heat, and washed away everything outside of their hot, wet cocoon. Nikos washed her carefully, thoroughly, as if she were something indescribably precious.

Not precious, she reminded herself. *Merely a possession. He is a man who takes good care of his possessions.*

He did not speak as he washed her, and he did not speak when he pulled her from the shower's warmth and dried her, still so carefully, with towels as soft as clouds. He pulled the fluffy cotton around her, and their eyes caught. His gaze was serious, more brown than gold. She had never felt more naked, more vulnerable. More exposed.

She had known from the moment she set eyes on him on the yacht that she should not—must not—allow this night to happen. And she had even known why. She had known that he would tear her into pieces, rip her open and leave her helpless. She could not handle this. Him. She had known all of that, and she had done it anyway.

The worst part was, even now, even knowing that she was in deeper trouble than she had ever been in before, she could not bring herself to regret it. Not a moment of it. Not even *this* moment. Biting her lip, she pulled the towel tighter across her breasts.

His eyes searched hers, then dropped to her mouth as if he, too, felt the pull of this impossible, incandescent attraction. But he did not act upon it. He merely ushered Tristanne into the other room, and into the vast bed that sat raised upon a dark marble platform.

Tristanne lay with her head nestled into his shoulder and wondered how she could ever, possibly, survive this. Survive him.

His hands stroked through her damp hair, as if learning the raw silk of its texture with his fingers. He sighed slightly, as if the same words bubbled up in him that she knew fought to escape her own mouth, though she bit them back, preserving the silence between them—knowing what would happen once the silence between them ended. What had to happen.

Words were the only weapon she had, and she had abandoned them entirely tonight. She could not understand why she had done so. Was it Peter? Had his nastiness finally proved too much for her? Had she been desperate for Nikos's touch because she wanted to prove, to herself at the least, that everything Peter said was a twisted lie? Or was it that Nikos was the only person who had ever made her feel safe in Peter's presence? Did she want all of this heat, all of this fire, to mean something more than she knew it could?

Tristanne was almost afraid to take the necessary steps back, to try to navigate their relationship now that it had gone so physical, so atomic. How would she handle what had happened between them, when she could still hardly manage to take a deep breath? How could it still be happening, even now?

She should have been exhausted, but instead she felt herself soften and grow restless as she lay against him, breathing in the dizzying, seductive scent of his warm skin. She felt that now familiar, but no less irresistible, fire move through her, making her limbs feel heavy, and her mouth go dry.

How could she want him, when she had already had him, and more than once? Something like anguish moved through her, mingling with the ever-present burn of desire, making her wonder what kind of sorcery this was—and how she would ever escape him. She knew, now, what it meant to be burned alive by this man. Before, she had only considered how he would ruin her. She had not imagined that she would crave the very thing that would destroy her, slowly and surely, with every touch of his hands and every tantalizing kiss.

She knew that he would haunt her for the rest of her days.

Perhaps that was why she turned her head, and pressed desperate kisses against his hard, wide chest, hardly understanding her own urges. Perhaps that was why the way his hand closed around the back of her neck was like gasoline against a flame, and his mouth against hers a bright new inferno. She could not help but surrender herself to the now-familiar, still-devastating whirl, the kick and the fire. She moved against him helplessly, wantonly, and then somehow she was astride him.

For a moment she looked down at him, and all she could see was the gold gleam of those eyes, and the wicked curve of his mouth as she took him deep inside of her.

She was irrevocably, irretrievably lost. In more ways than she could possibly count.

She had known it would be this way from the start. She had dreamed this when she was still just a girl, and had only imagined him from afar. *She had known.*

And so she moved against him, losing what was left of her in the glory of the fire that raged between them, not caring, in the dark of the night, that it left her little more than ash. Just as she had expected. Just as she had worried.

Exactly as she had feared.

CHAPTER ELEVEN

HIGH on the green and gray cliffs of Kefalonia, Tristanne sat out on the wide stone patio that encircled the sumptuous villa and let the wild, rugged coastline of the Greek island sink into her bones, as if the shining Ionian Sea could soothe her, somehow, as it crashed against the dark rocks far below. Olive groves, bursts of pine and columns of cypress trees lined the narrow isthmus that stretched out before her in the late morning light. The tiny fishing village of Assos straddled the small spit of land, cheerful orange roofs turned toward the sun, while the ruins of a sixteenth century Venetian palace stood sentry above. This was not the smooth, white and blue beauty of the better-known Greek islands that Tristanne had explored in her youth. This was tenacious, resilient Greece, beautiful for its craggy cliffs as well as its unexpected and often hidden golden-sand beaches.

It did not surprise her that this remote and isolated stretch of land, torn between the cliffs and the sea, was the place Nikos Katrakis called home.

Tristanne shifted in her seat, and deliberately did not look over her shoulder to where Nikos sat closer to the wide-open patio doors that led inside, taking one of his innumerable business calls on his mobile phone in clipped, impatient Greek. She did not have to look at him to know where he was and what he was doing. It was as if she had been tuned to him, on some kind of radio frequency that only she could hear. She knew when he was near. Her breasts tightened and her sex warmed, readying her body for him, no matter what.

It was only one among many reasons to despair, she knew. Only one among many reasons to accept that she had lost any measure of control she might have had over this odd interlude in her life. If there was any way she could have been further complicit in her own destruction, Tristanne could not imagine what that might be.

He had taken her over, body and soul. He made love to her so fiercely, so comprehensively, so well and so often, that she wondered how she would ever be the same again. She worried that she had completely lost touch with whoever she might have been before that night in Florence. And the most frightening part was that she was not at all certain she cared as she should, as she knew she had back in Florence, standing in that flat with the Duomo looming behind her, trying to stop the inevitable. The days turned to weeks, and she could do nothing but burn for him. Again and again and again.

They had sailed from Italy to Greece, stopping wherever the mood took them. Sorrento. Palermo. The sights blurred in her memory, narrowing to a singular focus. Nikos. She remembered his slow, hot smile on a sun-baked street in Sorrento. She remembered the possessive weight of his hand in the small of her back as they explored the old seawall in the ancient city of Valletta in Malta. Then they had sailed on to the famed island of Ithaka, before mooring in Assos, the small village on neighboring Kefalonia that Nikos called his home.

"The villa was originally my grandfather's," he'd said that first afternoon, when they'd left the yacht in the tiny harbor and were in the back of an exquisitely maintained Mercedes as it navigated the twisting, turning road toward the hills. "It came to me following my father's death."

"So you never came here as a child?" she had asked. She had been staring out the window of the car at the pebbled beach in the village center, where children played beneath white umbrellas, and the pastel facades of the houses seemed to beg to be photographed, all of it beneath the impossible blue of the Greek sky.

His look had been dark, and far too cynical to be amused.

"I did not holiday on the island, if that is what you mean. I grew up in Athens, and stayed there," he'd said, matter-of-factly, and she'd remembered, then, his talk of slums and poverty, and had flushed. It had already started then, she knew, the need she felt to protect him—even from his own past. She had not yet allowed herself to think about what that must mean—what it could not mean. What she refused to permit it to mean.

"Since you call it home, I assumed that meant you had some childhood connection to it," she had said stiffly. She was terrified that he could sense that she had softened considerably, that she *cared* in ways she knew perfectly well would appall him. It appalled her. His dark gaze had been cool, assessing, and she'd frozen next to him in the backseat of the old Mercedes that his servant drove carefully up the snaking, hilly road, hoping her expression would remain calm, removed.

"It is the only one of my father's properties that he never visited as long as I knew him," he'd said in that detached, cold way that did not encourage further discussion. "I suppose I find his absence soothing."

She had not asked any further questions about his father. Not then. He had swept her into the villa, and then into the wide bed in his stark white room that took its only color from the sea beyond, the stretch of water and the gleaming bowl of the endless sky. And she had been so hungry for him, so desperate to feel that heady rush and that exquisite fall into ecstasy, that she had not minded such diversions.

If only we could stay in bed forever, she thought now, her eyes on the horizon.

But once they were in Greece, where Nikos seemed to be as much a part of the island landscape as the olive trees and the rugged hills, it seemed almost inevitable that the old tycoon should come up in conversation. His father, she'd learned, had been raised on this island by Nikos's grandfather, then sent out into the world to help run the old man's business concerns. It was difficult to say which of those two men had been the harder, the more driven. She told herself she wanted to know about his family because it made sense to learn all she could about the man who had so entranced her, however brief this liaison must be, but she was afraid she knew perfectly well that was not the reason she asked.

"Did you know your grandfather?" she had asked one afternoon, as they sat in a bustling taverna in the village square lunching on goat *stifada* and fresh-grilled sea bass in a delectable lemon sauce. Tristanne sipped at a dry white wine while Nikos drank from a large glass of Mythos beer.

"You are obsessed with a man who has been dead for decades," Nikos had said in quelling tones. His brows had arched high, mocking her. "Are you looking for ghosts, Tristanne? The island is full of them, I am sure. There are plenty of saints and martyrs here to occupy your thoughts. There is no need to go digging in my history."

"I am hardly obsessed," she had replied in the calm voice that she wielded as her only remaining weapon. Her only armor, however weak. She'd taken a sip of her wine and had pretended to be unmoved. "I am interested, however. He built an amazingly artistic home for a man you refer to in such harsh terms." The villa was an artist's dream—every room carefully designed to captivate the senses, and to gracefully frame the stunning views.

"My grandfather was not a particularly nice man, Tristanne," Nikos had said, a gleam in his dark eyes that had made the fine hairs on the back of her neck prickle in warning. "And the only artistic impulse he possessed involved buying things that others told him were sought-after." He'd shrugged, though his gaze had been hard. "But what man who builds an empire is *nice*? He raised his son to be even worse. His own image, magnified." His mouth had twisted. "This is my heritage, of which I am deeply proud."

She'd let his sardonic tone wash over her, and schooled herself not to react. He would not respond well to any show of emotion, she knew—any hint of compassion, or identification. She'd sometimes thought he deliberately tested her to see if there was any hint of softness in her demeanor. It was her duty to behave as if all that was between them was sex and the promise of money. Perhaps, for him, that was even true.

"Whether you are proud of it or not," she had said then, "it is still where you come from. It is worth knowing."

"I know exactly where I come from," he had retorted in that quiet, dangerous tone that Tristanne remembered only too well from Portofino. Did it mean she had struck a nerve? Or only that he wished to slap her down, put her in her place? She'd felt her chin rise in automatic defense. His mocking half smile had seemed extra bitter then, as if he'd been able to read her as well as she was learning to read him.

"Then there is no need to get so upset about it, is there?" she had asked lightly.

His eyes had seemed to catch fire and his smile had deepened to a razor's point.

"Why should I be upset?" he had asked, in that cutting tone, though whether he'd wished to slice into her or himself, she'd been unable to tell. "In retrospect, I should thank my

father for casting my mother aside when her charms as a
mistress grew stale. After all, she was merely a dancer in a
club. What did he owe her? That he chose to favor her at all
was more than she could have dreamed. No doubt that is why
she succumbed to the usual narcotics, and abandoned me.
But then, as he told me himself many years later, long after
I proved myself to him through DNA and hard work—the
streets hardened me. Made me a more formidable opponent."
His shrug then had struck her as almost painful to watch.
"Truly, I should have thanked him while I had the chance."

"He sounds deeply unpleasant," Tristanne had said
quietly.

"He was Demetrios Katrakis," Nikos had said coldly.
"What softer feelings he had, and he did not have many, he
reserved for his late wife and their daughter. Not his gutter
trash bastard son." His expression had been so fierce then,
almost savage. Tristanne had known, somehow, that were
she to show even a hint of sympathy, he would never find it
in himself to forgive her.

So, instead, she had settled back in her seat, sipped at her
wine and gazed out at the picturesque little village, quite as
if her heart were not breaking into pieces inside her chest, for
the discarded little boy she knew he would never acknowledge had existed.

He never spoke of these conversations. He only made love
to her with an intensity that she worried, sometimes, in the
dark of night, might destroy them both. How could anyone
live with so much stark, impossible pleasure? How could
they handle so much fire so often, and not turn themselves
into cinders?

So rather than voice the thoughts and feelings that she
was afraid to entertain even in the sanctity of her own head,
Tristanne drew. She drew Nikos in a hundred poses, in a
hundred ways. She told herself he was no more and no less
than an example of a particular kind of hard male beauty,

and she owed it to her artistic growth to master his form with pencils and a pad of paper.

That was why she traced the line of his nose a thousand times, the high thrust of his cheekbones, the proud set of his chin. That was why she agonized over the fullness of his lips, so wicked and seductive even at his most mocking, his most cutting. She spent whole afternoons learning the sweep of his magnificent torso; spent endless hours studying the strength and cleverness of his hands. It was to improve her craft, she told herself—to become a better artist.

"Surely you have drawn me more than enough," Nikos said now, coming to stand behind her. His fingers moved through her hair, pulling at the dark blonde waves almost absently. "Why not sketch the rocks? The cliffs? The cypress trees?"

Tristanne had not heard him end his call, but she had known the moment he moved across the wide patio to join her. She sat on one of the comfortable chairs that was placed to take advantage of the sweeping views of the Assos peninsula and the Ionian Sea beyond. But on the pad propped up on her knees in front of her was another drawing of Nikos. This time, she had drawn him in profile, his brow furrowed in thought, his mouth curled down at the corners. This was the Nikos she knew all too well, she thought now, looking at the drawing with a practiced eye. Resolute. Commanding. In control.

"I prefer to draw people—it's far more challenging. And you are the only person I see regularly," she said airily. "I could ask one of the tourists in the village to pose for me, but I do not believe you would care for it if I did."

"Indeed, I would not." There was an undercurrent of amusement in his rich voice, and she knew if she looked that he would be biting back that almost-smile.

"So, you see, I must use you," she said. "It is an artistic imperative."

She put down her pencil, and twisted to look up at him. As ever, her breath caught in her throat as she gazed at him. As ever, he seemed larger-than-life, blocking out the enormous azure sky. She could not see the gold in his eyes with his face in shadow, but she felt it anyway, as if another kind of gold hummed within her, and turned into an electric current when he touched her.

"I must go into Athens this afternoon," he said in a low voice. His hand moved from her hair to her cheek. His thumb traced a firm line along her jaw.

"Do I accompany you?" she asked softly. She could not pretend that she was not his mistress now, in word and in deed. Not when she knew what to ask and how to ask it, with no expectation or recrimination. Only availability. She was endlessly, terrifyingly available. She told herself that she was only ensuring Peter's continued compliance, and thus her mother's future, as they came ever closer to the month her brother had demanded at the party in Florence. Peter had even sent the papers that indicated she would have access to her trust, should she continue as she was. She was not doing this on a whim, she reminded herself firmly. Her plan was working just as she'd hoped. She had not meant to sleep with Nikos, it was true, nor had she anticipated spending more than a few days with him, but the fact that those things had changed did not alter the rest of her plans in any respect. She was not like her mother in her earlier, healthier days, kept for a man's pleasure like an inanimate object; a toy. She was not. She told herself so every day.

"I will only be gone a few hours," he said. He meant he would take the helicopter, which made the trip to his office in Athens merely a long, if rather flamboyant commute. "I will return tonight."

"I will miss you, then," she said, in that casual tone that she knew would not set off his alarms. She was so calm, so blasé. She worked so hard to appear that way. "Luckily I have my drawings of you. In case I begin to forget what you look like."

He pulled her to her feet, sliding a hand around to the small of her back and holding her against his wide chest. He looked down into her face. She felt the heat of his hand seep into her skin, warming her, even as she felt the usual quickening within. She did not know what his expression meant—only that he searched her own, and that his eyes burned into hers.

Did he know? she wondered in a sudden panic. *Had she somehow given herself away?*

"Perhaps you can help me pack," he murmured suggestively.

Because that was the only fire they acknowledged, the only way they could.

She hid the rest of it. Sometimes even from herself.

"Of course," she said, like the perfect mistress she was more and more these days. Just as she'd always feared. Just as Peter had predicted. She smiled at him. "I can think of nothing I would rather do."

Because she knew beyond the slightest doubt that she could not tell him that she loved him. She could not. She could never tell him that she loved him—she could not even think the words, for fear they would bleed onto her tongue without her knowledge.

She could only love him with her body, and the soft strokes and broad lines of her pencils, and pray with all she had that he never, ever knew.

Nikos strode through the villa, his temper igniting with every step.

She was nowhere to be found. She was not lounging suggestively in his bed, wearing something appropriately saucy. She was not taking a coincidentally perfectly timed shower, the better to lure him in. She was not in any number of places she could have been in—should have been in—and the fact that he had rushed home from Athens to see her made him more furious about her deficiencies as a mistress than he might have been otherwise.

A man should not have to hunt down his mistress. A man should simply cross the threshold and find her waiting there, beautiful and sweet-smelling, with a soft smile on her lips and a cold drink in her hand.

Nikos stopped on the patio, and scowled at the sun as it sank toward the horizon, spilling red and pink fingers over the gleaming sea. It infuriated him how often he seemed to forget the fact that Tristanne was not, in point of fact, his mistress. He was no better than a boy, letting his head get turned by scaldingly hot sex. It had taken today's meeting with his team in his office to reacquaint himself with his goals: Peter Barbery, as expected, was trading on Nikos's good name with all manner of investors, Nikos's people had confirmed. Apparently the man's personal loathing of Nikos would not prevent Peter from acting as if the two of them were thick as thieves. Which meant that everything was in place. All that Nikos needed to do now was up the stakes. Raise the bar just that little bit higher, so when he sent it all crashing down, it would really, truly hurt. Leave scars, even.

And he knew just how to do it.

He had rushed back to the island, telling himself that he was not *excited* to do this thing so much as finally recommitted to his original vision of how this entire operation would proceed. He had lost his focus slightly, he had admitted to himself on the helicopter ride from Athens. Tristanne was a beautiful woman, and he was a man who greatly appreciated beauty, especially when he found it wrapped around him every morning like a vine. More than that, she grew more mysterious by the day, and he found he was more and more intrigued by his sense that she was hiding more than she shared. But this, he had concluded today, was simply because he wondered what the Barberys' end game was; what they thought they could gain from him.

He would accept no other reason for his uncharacteristic obsession with this woman. There was no room for anything but his revenge, surely.

He heard a scuffing sound then, and turned to see Tristanne emerge from the bushes that marked the edge of the cliff. She held her drawing pad in one hand, and looked at the ground as she walked. Her hair was twisted back into one of those smooth, efficient knots he hated, and she wore rolled up denim trousers, thronged-sandals, and an oversize shirt. She looked like a local painter, not a beguiling mistress—and she did not seem to notice that he was standing there, watching her approach.

Of course. Why had he expected anything different?

He told himself that what he felt was annoyance. Irritation that she should be so desperately inept. He told himself that he was simply shocked that she was so ill equipped to play her own game of deception.

"Look at you," he said coolly, his low voice rolling through the falling dark and wrenching her head up. "Have you been climbing up and down the cliffs? You look bedraggled enough to have attempted it."

"Not at all," she said as she closed the distance between them. Her chin, as ever, firmed and rose. The frown that had dented the space between her brows disappeared as her eyebrows arched. "Did you not indicate earlier that you preferred me to draw inanimate objects? I was merely obeying you. Rocks. Trees. As ordered."

The sarcastic inflection to her voice infuriated him. The defiant gleam in her brown eyes, reflecting the last red streaks of the sunset, provoked him. She should have been begging, pleading, *insinuating* herself. Wasn't that why she was here in the first place? Instead she had challenged him from the start. She did it even now. He was not even sure she did it deliberately.

She was *naturally* provoking.

"You," he said coldly, "are very possibly the worst mistress in the history of the world."

CHAPTER TWELVE

His words seemed to hang there in the dusk, swirling around them both like the sea air and the sound of the waves against the base of the cliffs far below. He did not know why he felt his heart pound so hard against his chest, much less why he felt himself harden.

"I beg your pardon," Tristanne said, her eyes throwing daggers at him. He watched her shoulders tense and then square. "I had no idea I was so deficient."

"Now you do." He swept his gaze over her. "What do you call this ensemble, Tristanne?"

She stiffened, and her free hand curled over into a fist before she shoved it into her pocket. "I believe the word I would choose is *comfortable*," she said, very precisely.

"*Comfortable* is not a word in a mistress's vocabulary." He shook his head at her. "Unless you are referring to my comfort. I expected to enter this villa and find you arrayed in front of me, like a banquet for my eyes."

"Are you sure you are discussing a mistress?" Tristanne asked in the same irritatingly cool, calm tone. "Because it sounds to me as if you are referring to a pack mule. Or the family hound."

"You are argumentative," Nikos said, as if he were checking off a list. "Independent." She blinked, and then averted her gaze, and he hated it. "Unacceptably mysterious," he gritted out.

"You will find, I think, that those are characteristics of most adults," Tristanne said. She moved to the nearby table and set her pad down upon it. "Perhaps you do not encounter such creatures in your daily attempts to rule the world, but I assure you, they are out there."

"And you are too clever by half," he replied in a silky tone. "And do not mistake me, Tristanne. That is not a compliment."

She turned toward him then, something he could not understand moving quickly across her face, gone in an instant. Was it…a kind of grief? But that made no sense.

"You will have to excuse my ignorance," she said, a storm brewing in her gaze, though no hint of it touched her voice. "I thought that your initial objections to my concept of my role as your mistress centered entirely on whether or not we would fall into bed. Having answered that question, in a way that I am quite certain is to your satisfaction, I fail to see how anything else matters."

"You fight with me at the slightest provocation," he said as if she hadn't spoken. As if he did not want to explore the satisfaction to which she had just referred, despite his body's instant and enthusiastic reaction. He crossed his arms over his chest as he looked down at her, enjoying himself. "How is this proper behavior? How is this enticing?"

At that, she actually laughed. "You are claiming that you do not find it enticing?" she asked. "My mistake. I thought your preferred method for conflict resolution proved otherwise."

Just yesterday she had argued with him about something absurd—some take on an article in the local paper—and he had had her there in the infinity pool while the sun beat down on them and birds called to each other from above, rendering them both happily wordless. *Conflict resolution*, indeed.

He could not help but smile.

"My point is that you do not suit as a mistress," he said. "How could you? I should have known when you asked for the position that it could never work."

"And why is that?" she asked, a hint of pink high on her cheeks.

"Because women do not *ask* to become my mistress," he said softly. "Why should they? They either are, or are not. It is always quite clear." He was fascinated by the ruthless way she kept her expression under control. Only a twitch near her eyes, and the faintest tremble of her lips betrayed her. "And I am the one to do the asking."

"I believe I get your point," she said crisply. "There is no need to belabor it. What is next, Nikos? A play-by-play breakdown of every time we—"

"You do not get my point." He interrupted her, his gaze hard on her face. "I am only stating a fact, which should in no way surprise you. Do you think I did not know perfectly well that you had no interest at all in becoming my mistress?"

She seemed to freeze then.

"I don't know what you mean," she said after a moment. He suspected that if she were another kind of woman, she might have stammered.

"You do." He arched a brow. "But you need not concern yourself, Tristanne. I know what you wanted."

She swallowed. "You do?" Her chin rose. "You must enlighten me. I thought I was perfectly clear about what I wanted. And perfectly satisfied with the result."

He let the moment drag out, enjoying himself far too much. He loved the panic that flashed in her gaze before she shuttered it, the nervousness she betrayed by the smallest of gestures—*almost* shifting her weight from foot to foot, *almost* biting her lower lip.

"I cannot have you as my mistress any longer, Tristanne," he said quietly. "You are terrible at it."

"Very well," she said, her voice even, her eyes carefully

blank. He wondered what that cost her. "I am devastated, of course."

He almost laughed at the insulting blandness she managed to inject into that last line—a fighter until the end, this woman. She would go down swinging, or die trying. He could not help but admire the sheer force of her bravado. It reminded him of his own bullheadedness, back in his angry youth.

"You are an idiot," he said then. He shook his head at her. "I am not casting you aside."

"Are you certain of that?" she asked dryly. Something flashed in her eyes. Relief? Irritation? "The recitation of my many flaws and the myriad ways I have disappointed you seems to suggest otherwise. Or perhaps this is the Nikos Katrakis brand of affection? How delightful."

"You cannot help yourself, can you?" he asked, his voice almost mild. He moved closer to her, then reached over to trace the mouth that spat such foolishness at him, the mouth that poked at him and exasperated him—the mouth that he found himself fantasizing about when she was not in the room. "You will keep going until you drop, no matter the cost to you."

She did not jerk her head back from his touch, nor shiver beneath his hand, but he had the sense that she fought off both. Her gaze searched his.

"I don't understand this conversation," she said quietly.

And then, he could put it off no longer. He felt something powerful move through him. *Revenge*, he told himself. Finally he would have his revenge. But it felt much more like a necessity than a tactic or a strategy—though he refused to consider why that might be.

"Marry me," he said.

"Oh," she managed to say somehow, her mind reeling, while her heart galloped wildly in her chest. Did she fall back a few steps? Had she fainted? But no, she was still standing there on the patio, too warm from her hike back up the side of the cliff—and from Nikos's unexpected, scowling appearance.

Or perhaps the heat that washed over her had more to do with what he had just said.

"I will not get on my knees, Tristanne," he told her in his infuriatingly arrogant way. He looked almost amused at the thought. "Nor will I spontaneously burst into poetry."

She could not think. She could not *think*, and that was the danger, because if she could not think, she could only feel... and she did not want to feel the things she felt. She could not allow herself to feel the emotions that coursed through her, buffeting her, as if she were no more substantial than a leaf in high winds.

A fierce, overwhelming joy suffused her, pulsing through her veins, blocking out the world for a moment—blocking out reality. The tantalizing idea, as painful as it was inviting, that she could have this man—really have him, when she knew she could not—called to a deep well of hope she had not known she held inside. But oh, the joy of imagining, even for a second, that she was not deceiving him! That he was proposing to a woman who actually existed—instead of this fake mistress person she had tried so hard to put on, like a second skin. He thought she was a failure at it, but then, he had no idea how far from herself she'd had to go to get here.

He had no idea.

"If I were someone else," he drawled then, his dark eyes a harder version of amused, "I might be rendered insecure by your continued silence."

But her mind was still racing, her heart still pounding— and she was frozen solid. Peter, she knew, would exult in this opportunity. Marrying Tristanne off to a rich man he could then lean on for financial support was an abiding fantasy of his; their father had shared it. It would solve all of her problems. Nikos would help her help her mother, of course, and Vivienne would finally be debt-free and on the way to recovery. Tristanne would be free of Peter, finally, for she could not imagine that her brother would bother with her any longer if he could approach Nikos directly. If he dared.

If only she did not love him.

"I can see your brain working overtime," Nikos said, tilting his head slightly as he gazed down at her. "What can there be to think about, Tristanne? We both know there can be only one answer."

If only she did not love him.

But she did love him, every arrogant, demanding, exasperating inch of him. She loved the way he moved through the world, using that powerful body and his far more impressive mind to cut a swathe before him. She loved the way he held her so tenderly sometimes, though she knew he would deny any and all softer emotions—or any emotions at all—were she to say such a thing aloud. She loved the defiant way he spoke of his past, as if it did not hurt him, as if it had not shaped him. *She loved.* She loved with every breath, with every caress of pencil against paper, with every touch of skin to skin. She loved him more than she had ever loved another person in her life, more than she could ever say, and she knew that she could not marry him. Not when almost everything she'd said to him, more or less, was a lie.

He had not spoken of love, she knew, nor would he. But did that matter? She knew the truths between them that only their bodies could speak. He did not have to feel as she did. She was not certain that he could, even if he'd wanted to do something so anathema to him.

Which only made it more clear what she must do, though every part of her rebelled. Every cell rose up in revolt, almost choking her to keep her from saying what she resolved she must say. She felt a sharp heat behind her eyes, but she would not cry. She would not.

"I cannot marry you," she said at last, the words ripped from her, seeming to tear at her throat, her tongue, her lips. She was not sure how she managed to do it. But she could not lie to the man she loved, not any longer. She simply could not. She would find some other way to save her mother, somehow, but she could not do this anymore. The fact that she had done it at all was something she would regret for the rest of her days.

"No?" He did not seem particularly taken aback by her declaration. "Are you certain? I feel sure that you can."

"I mean that I *will not* marry you," she amended, with every last drop of bravado she possessed. As if it did not kill her to say it. As if it were not a supreme act of sacrifice to say such a thing to him when she knew, she just *knew*, that she could love enough for both of them. She could feel the force of it, thudding heavy and hard against the walls of her chest.

"Ah." He studied her. "Have you gone over all romantic, Tristanne? Has talk of marriage led you to fantasize about notions of forever and matching rings?" He laughed, shortly. "I assure you, I will have my lawyers bury us both in prenuptial contracts. I imagine that will prove a cure for any lingering romantic fantasies."

"That would be a relief, I am sure," Tristanne somehow brought herself to say, even managing a certain level of dryness. As if she could be as cynically detached as he was—as he expected her to be.

"Then what is your objection to my proposal?" He shrugged with the supreme confidence of a man who knew himself to be one of the world's greatest catches, wanted by untold numbers of women on innumerable continents. "You cannot say we do not suit."

"You just spent some time detailing the ways in which we do not suit," Tristanne said, almost testily. She did not know why she continued to spar with him. She should simply leave him, she knew. She should do it now, while she still felt virtuous for refusing him. Before the pain caught up with her and laid her out, flat, as she suspected it would. As she feared it would.

She had always known he would haunt her—and that was before she'd been foolish enough to fall head over heels in love with her.

"A man does not expect to argue with his mistress," Nikos said, his mocking half smile appearing again. "But that is the province of a wife, is it not?"

"I do not think you believe half of the things that come out of your mouth," Tristanne threw at him, fighting the swell of her own emotions. She wanted, too badly, to be the woman she'd pretended to be. The woman he'd actually proposed to, instead of the woman she was. "I think you simply say these things for effect!"

"Marry me, and see for yourself," he suggested, completely unperturbed. Daring her, in fact, to marry him!

Tristanne felt something break inside of her, and had to bite back a gasp that she feared would come out more of a sob. She could not cry. She *would not* cry, not now, not in front of him. But she felt all of her fight, all of the bravado she'd clung to as her only defense against this man, go out of her in a great rush.

What was she fighting for? Why was she being so noble? The truth was that she was selfish, not sacrificing, because she wanted to say yes more than she could remember wanting anything else, ever. She wanted to disappear completely into the life that Nikos offered her, and bury herself in the sizzling heat of his embrace. The truth was that she loved Nikos, and while it was something Peter could never possibly understand, she knew in her heart that her mother would. And how could she walk away from him without even trying to tell him the truth about herself? How would she ever manage to live with herself if she did such a thing?

She loved him, for all she knew that such a thing was neither wise nor rational, and she had to believe that somewhere inside of him, buried beneath all those layers of masculine pride and years of neglect and solitude, he felt something for her. Surely she had to trust him enough to tell him the truth, if she had any hope at all of trusting him with her heart—or, at the very least, of surviving this relationship with him with any part of herself intact.

She let her fists clench at her sides. She stood straight. She raised her head high, and she looked him straight in the eye. She let his old gold gaze warm her, and she refused to let herself give in to the heat that prickled behind her eyes.

"I cannot marry you," she said quietly, with as much dignity as she could muster, "because I am lying to you. I have been lying to you from the start."

CHAPTER THIRTEEN

"HAVE you?" Nikos sounded almost offhand, very nearly bored, as if people confessed to deceiving him several times a day. Perhaps they did, Tristanne thought ruefully. Or, much more likely, this show of nonchalance was carefully calibrated to disarm the unwary so he might strike when they least expected it.

"I have," she said. She studied his dark face. The haughty cheekbones, the full mouth pulled into its characteristic smirk. She wanted to press herself against the heat of him; lose herself in the heady passion that only he had ever aroused in her. But she had already lost too much of herself in this terrible game, so she merely waited.

"Come," Nikos drawled after a long moment. "We will have some wine and sit, like civilized people, and you will tell me how you have lied to me for all of this time."

Bemused, Tristanne could do nothing but follow Nikos inside. He poured himself a glass of wine from the bar in the corner of the living room, and merely shrugged when Tristanne refused one for herself. The tasteful room was all done in whites and neutral colors that inexorably led the eye to the spectacular view, visible through the floor-to-ceiling glass on three sides. He settled himself into one of the low-slung armchairs and raised a brow, inviting her to continue.

Tristanne laced her fingers together before her, and

frowned down at her clasped hands. She could not bring herself to sit down, as if they were having cocktails and everything was perfectly normal. She did not feel civilized in any respect. Her heart beat too fast, and she felt too hot, too restless. Dizzy. She wished she could go back in time and keep herself from speaking at all. She should have either accepted his proposal, or simply said no and left it at that. Why was she exposing herself like this? What was there to gain? He was so remote, so cold now—sitting there as if they hardly knew each other. And she was making it worse by dithering over it, dragging the uncomfortable silence out…

"I remembered you," she said, not knowing what she planned to say until it was out there, hanging in the air of the elegant room while the Greek night pressed against the windows, dark and rich. "I saw you at a ball in my father's home when I was still a girl. I mention this because it was the first lie, that I saw you for the first time on your yacht that day."

He took a sip of his wine, then lounged back against his chair. His eyes were so dark, yet still shone of gold. She took that as a good sign—or, at least, not a negative one. Not yet.

And so she told him. She stood like a penitent before a king, and she confessed every part of it. Peter's mismanagement of the family finances and her mother's frailty and ill health. Her need for her trust fund in order to settle her mother's debts and take her somewhere safer and better, which Tristanne felt she owed her. Peter's revolting ultimatums, and his obsessive hatred of Nikos, which had been one of the reasons she'd picked him. The things Peter had said about Nikos, and about Tristanne, and what she knew Peter hoped to gain from her liaison with Nikos. What she had expected to gain from her association with Nikos, and how surprised she had been by the passion that had flared between them.

She talked and she talked, a ball of dread growing larger

and heavier in her gut with each word. As she spoke, Nikos hardly moved. He drank from his wineglass from time to time, but otherwise merely listened, stretched out in his chair with his hard face completely unreadable, propped up against one hand.

She realized that she had no idea what he would do. He was a ruthless, dangerous man—she had known that from the start, hadn't she? It was why she'd chosen him. She had no doubt that he dealt with betrayal harshly. Like the dragon he was. What would he do to her?

When she was finished, she found herself staring down at her hands once more. She willed herself not to shake. Not to weep. Not to beg or plead with him. And not, under any circumstances, to let it slip that she was in love with him. She nearly shuddered then, at the very thought. She did not have to know what would happen next to know *that* would be like throwing gasoline on an open flame.

"And this is why you say you will not marry me?"

Her head shot up at the sound of his low, firm voice. She searched his face, but could see nothing save that same fire in his gaze. She could only nod, no longer trusting herself to speak.

Nikos leaned forward, and set his wine down on the wide glass coffee table. As Tristanne watched, panic and hope and fear surged through her in equal measure, making her feel light-headed. He stood up with that masculine grace that, even now, made her throat go dry.

"I do not care," he said quietly, fiercely, closing the distance between them. He reached over and cupped her cheek in his hand, his eyes dark and intense. "I do not care about any of it."

"What?" She could barely speak. Her voice was a thread of sound, and she knew she was trembling, shaking—finally breaking down in front of him, as she had vowed she would never do. *Must* never do! "How can you say such a thing? Of course you must care!"

"I care that you have been put in a position to do such things by your pig of a brother," he growled at her, his voice low and rough, as if he, too, did not entirely trust himself to speak. "I care that had I refused your proposition, you might have made it to someone else." His hand, hot against her skin, tightened a fraction. "I care that you are standing before me trying your hardest not to weep."

"I am not!" she snapped at him, but it was too late. She felt all of her fear, all of her anger and pain and isolation and love, so much desperate, impossible love, coalesce into that searing heat in her eyes and then spill over, tracking wet, hot tears down her face.

She disgraced herself, and yet she could not seem to stop.

He murmured something in Greek, something tender, and it made it all the worse. Tristanne jabbed at her eyes with the back of one hand, furious at herself. What was next? Would she start to cling to the hem of his trousers as he made for the door? How soon would she become her mother, in every aspect?

It was a chilling thought. Her very worst nightmare made real—but then Nikos took her face in both of his hands, and she could think only of him.

"Listen to me," he said, in that supremely arrogant way of his—that tone that demanded instant obedience. "You will marry me. I will handle your brother, and your mother will be protected. You will not worry about any of this again. Do you understand me?"

"You cannot order me to marry you," she said, pricked into remembering her own spine by the sheer conceit of him, by his overwhelming confidence that her very tears would dry up on the spot at his command.

His hands tightened slightly, and his mouth curved into a very male smile.

"I just did," he said. "And you will."

And then he kissed her, as if it was all a foregone conclusion; as if she had already agreed.

She could have been putting on an elaborate act, but he did not think so, Nikos thought much later as he stood out on the balcony that hung high over the cliffs, far above the crashing waves. He did not believe that her body could deceive him on that level, even if she wished it to do so.

He turned to look at her, stretched out across the rumpled bed inside the master suite, her eyes closed and her mouth slightly open as she slept. Her hair was a satisfying tangle around her shoulders, and her curves seemed to gleam in the moonlight—beckoning him with a siren's call he could not seem to escape. He felt himself stir, always ready for her, always desperate to lose himself inside her once again. He felt something squeeze tight inside of his chest, and turned his back on her again, ruthlessly.

The night was cool, with a brisk breeze coming in off the sea, smelling of salt and pine. Nikos stared out at the dark swell of the water and the twinkling lights of the village below, and could not understand why he did not feel that kick of adrenaline, that hum in his veins of victory firmly within his grasp. He had felt it when he'd weakened the various Barbery assets enough that, following the old man's death, it had taken the merest whisper to send them tumbling. He had celebrated that victory—remembering too well what it had been like when the situations were reversed and it had been the Katrakis fortune on the line. He remembered Peter's gloating laughter when he'd called to announce the deal was off, the Katrakis money lost, Althea discarded, and all of it according to the Barberys' plan. Nikos imagined the Barberys had celebrated that, too, all those years ago. He had made himself coldly furious over the years, imagining that very celebration in minute detail, reliving Peter's vile words.

So why did he not now feel as he should? He had reeled her in, completely. He had been astonished when she'd made her confession to him, though he could not allow himself to speculate too much on what might have led her to unburden herself. He could only think of a handful of motivations, none of them coming from places he wished to think about. What was important, he told himself, was that she'd told him everything there was to tell about her brother's plans. About her own part in those plans. And then she had made love to him like a wild thing, untamed and ravenous, moving over him in the dark of the bedroom as if she were made of fire and need, bringing them both to writhing ecstasy.

But Nikos did not feel that cool beat of triumph—he felt something else, something elemental and dark. Something wholly unfamiliar. Some deep-seated streak of possessiveness rose in him, roaring through him, making him question the scheme he had committed himself to so long ago.

You never meant to involve the girl, he reminded himself now, as if he still had a conscience. As if he had not rid himself of that encumbrance long since, as his actions with Tristanne made perfectly clear. *You never meant to do what Peter did.*

He thought of Althea then. Beautiful, impetuous, foolish Althea. His half sister by blood, though she claimed no particular family relationship to him unless it suited her purposes. He had been something like her bodyguard and her convenient escort, when she did not wish to be seen on the arm of their grizzled old father. And he, damn him, had been so desperate for her favor, for her approval. He had wanted to protect her, to make her smile, to prove to her that he deserved to call himself her brother even while their father treated him like the unwelcome hired help.

But she had not been interested in her feral half brother.

She had not cared if he stayed to ingratiate himself with their father or if he disappeared back into the ghetto from whence he came. If anything, she had resented the fact that she was no longer the sole focus of their father's attention—and even if what attention Demetrios Katrakis gave to his bastard son was negative, it was attention. She had not minded that Nikos was there, necessarily, but nor would she have cared particularly if he was not. Her indifference had only made him that much more determined to win her over.

But then she had fallen madly in love with Peter Barbery, and had sealed all of their fates.

Nikos let his hands rest on the rail in front of him, and forced himself to breathe. What was done was done, and there could be no undoing it. Peter had tossed Althea aside the moment Gustave Barbery had succeeded in cheating Demetrios out of a major deal. The entire Katrakis legacy had faltered. Althea had killed herself, and when it was found that she had been pregnant, Demetrios had blamed Nikos even more. For failing to protect her and the child? For surviving? Nikos had never known. A year later, Demetrios, too, had died, leaving Nikos to pick up the pieces of the Katrakis shipping empire.

It had all happened so fast. He had only just found his family, and the Barberys had ripped them away from him, one by one.

What was done was done, he repeated to himself. And what would be, would be. He had vowed it over his father's grave, and he was a man who kept his promises. Always.

But still, he did not feel that surge of cold certainty that had led him here. That focus and intensity that had allowed him to plot and plan from afar, across years. Was it because, as a little voice in the back of his head insisted, doing what he planned to do to Tristanne made him exactly like Peter Barbery? Worse, even—for Barbery had promised Althea nothing, while Nikos had every intention of abandoning Tristanne at the altar.

He could see it play out in his mind's eye, shot for shot, like he watched it in the cinema. Tristanne would walk down the aisle, dressed in something white and gauzy and ineffably lovely, and he would not be there. He would never be there. She would not cry, not in front of so many. He knew that the fact she'd cried in front of him tonight meant things he was unwilling to look at closely. But she would not cry in her moment of greatest humiliation. He could see, as if she stood before him, that strong chin rise into the air, and the tremor across her lips that she suppressed in an instant. He saw the smooth, calm expression she turned toward the crowd, toward the cameras, toward the gossip and the speculation.

And he saw the great bleakness in her chocolate eyes, that he feared she would never be rid of again.

He hissed out a harsh curse and let the night wind toss it toward the rocks far below, battering it into a million pieces.

This was different, he told himself fiercely. He had never intended to use Tristanne; she had approached him. How was he to refuse to use the perfect tool when it fell into his lap? After all this time? He thought of that odd, tender moment in the rain in Florence. He had been trying to forget it ever since it had happened. He was not like Peter Barbery, he told himself, even though he had the strangest feeling that when he did this thing to Tristanne, when he wounded her so deeply, so irrevocably—it might even wound him, too.

He, who had shut off that part of himself so long ago now that it was almost shocking to recall how much he had loved his spoiled, careless half sister, and how much it had hurt when she'd thrown that in his face. He had never thought anything could hurt him again.

"You are nothing to me!" she'd screamed at him when he'd attempted to console her after Peter's vicious termination of their relationship. He had not known, then, that she was pregnant. That Peter Barbery had scoffed at her and called her a whore—then claimed his own child could have been anyone's. All Nikos had known was that Althea had been in a lump on the floor of her room in their father's elegant mansion in Kifissia, her face streaked with tears. Still, her eyes, as they focused on him, were narrow and mean. Like their father's.

"Althea," he had said, his hands in the air, trying to soothe her. He had thought he had shown her that he was trustworthy—the older brother she had never had. Someone she could love and lean on. That was what he'd wanted.

"I wish you had never been born!" she had thrown at him, cutting him as surely as if she'd thrown a knife. "This is your fault! You were the one who was too cocky, too sure—"

"I will make this right," he had promised her. "I will. I swear it on my honor."

"Your honor? What is that to me?" She had been scornful then, her pretty face twisted, spiteful. "You may have climbed out of the sewer, Nikos, but you still walk around with the stench of it clinging to you, don't you? And you always will!"

Nikos shook the unpleasant memory away, gritting his teeth. Only a week later, she had been gone, her pregnancy uncovered. So much lost. So much wasted.

The Barberys deserved whatever they got, even Tristanne, the innocent one. He would not feel guilty for it.

He would not.

She was still half-asleep when he pulled her into his arms. Tristanne came awake as his body moved over hers, her own already responding to him, already softening for him, before she was fully aware of what was happening.

"You have yet to answer me," he said softly, moving his

mouth along the column of her neck. "I presume this is merely an oversight."

"What if my answer remains no?" she said, her voice husky from sleep, and, she thought, the fact that no secrets remained between them. Not any longer. She felt...naked unto her soul. New.

Vulnerable.

A faint memory stirred then, of Peter in Florence, asking snidely after Nikos's angle in all of this. She shook it away, concentrating instead on the feel of Nikos's hard muscles beneath her hands, his hot mouth against her skin, her breast. What could she do? She had told him everything. She could only hope that he would do her the same courtesy—but even if he did not, it was not as if she could simply decide to stop loving him in the meantime.

Her body would not allow her to stop wanting him, not even for the barest moment.

"Yes," she said, as he twisted his hips slightly and thrust deep into her, making her sigh with wonder at the perfect, slick fit.

"Yes, what?" he taunted her as, slowly, he began to move, stroking in and out of her, sending shivers of delight all through her limbs.

"You are a bully," she said, gasping.

"I am merely emphatic," he growled against her throat, nipping at her. "And very, very focused."

And because she could do nothing else, because ripples of pleasure fogged her brain and coursed through her veins, she wrapped her legs around him and held on tight.

His eyes were dark, threaded through with gold, and yet seemed almost conflicted as they met hers. He dropped his gaze, and kissed her, taking her mouth with an intensity she might have called desperate in another man. He began to thrust faster, harder, holding her bottom in his strong hands to please them both with the deeper angle.

"Yes," she said, because she could not remember, now, why she had denied him. She wanted to soothe him, to ease the darkness in his gaze. She *wanted*. "I will marry you."

He did not speak again. He merely lowered his head, and then he took them both over the edge.

CHAPTER FOURTEEN

"WE MUST marry quickly," Nikos said the following evening as they sat in the fading light, startling Tristanne as she feasted on tangy kalamata olives and sharp feta drenched in locally grown olive oil and spices. The sun had only just ducked below the horizon, and Nikos had only just returned from another day in Athens.

Part of her, she realized now, had wondered if the events of the previous night were real—of if she'd dreamed them. His words sent a thrill of anticipation through her.

"Why must we do anything of the kind?" she asked. "Surely we can have the usual engagement period. We would not want to suggest that there is any reason to rush, would we?"

"Will this turn into another battle, Tristanne?" he asked, his mouth curving into that familiar half smile, though there was a hardness to it tonight. "Will you explain to me what will and will not happen, at great length, only to acquiesce to my wishes in the end? Is that not the pattern?"

She wished there was not that edge to his voice, as if he meant his words on several levels she could not quite understand. She wished she did not feel slapped down, somehow. But she reminded herself that everything between them was different now. She had come clean and even so, he wanted to marry her.

Or so she kept telling herself, as if it were a mantra.

"Why do you wish to marry quickly?" she asked calmly, as if she had not noticed any edge, or even his usual sardonic inflection.

His dark eyes touched on hers, then dropped to caress her lips, then her breasts beneath the light cotton shift she wore. She ordered herself not to squirm in her seat; not to respond. Her body, as ever, reacted only to Nikos and ignored her entirely.

"Must you ask?" His voice was low. "Can you not tell?"

"I do not believe in divorce," she said quietly, holding his gaze when he looked at her again. She did not know why she felt compelled to say such a thing, even while her heart fluttered wildly in her chest. "I realize it is unfashionable to say so, but I have never understood the point of getting married at all if one does so with an escape clause."

"I assure you, divorce exists." He shook his head, and reached for one of the spicy olives. He popped it into his mouth. "My grandfather divorced three wives in his time."

"Especially not if there are children," she continued, ignoring him. She shrugged. "I have seen too many children destroyed in their parents' petty little wars. I could not do that to my own."

Something in his gaze went electric then, making her breath catch.

"If there are children," he said quietly, fiercely, "they will be born with my name and live under my protection. Always."

He did not speak for a long while then, looking out to sea instead. Something about the remoteness of his expression made her heart ache for him, for the abandoned child he had been, though she dared not express her sympathy. She was too worried he would read into it what should not be there—her unreasonable empathy, her compassion, the love she felt for him that scared her, on some level, with its absoluteness. Its certainty. It was a hard rock of conviction inside of her, for all that so much about him remained a mystery—as out of reach as the stars that shone ever brighter above her in the darkening sky.

Was it love? she wondered. Or was she deluding herself in a different way now? First she had thought she could maneuver around this man, use him for her own ends. That had proved laughable. Now she thought she could love him and make a marriage between them work based on only her love, and their breathtaking, consuming chemistry? Was she as foolish as the waves in the sea far below her, thinking they would remain intact as they threw themselves upon the rocks?

Did she really want to know?

"We will marry in two weeks," he said at last. His head turned toward her, his expression almost grim. "Here. If that suits you."

"Are you asking my opinion?" she asked dryly, as if things were as they'd used to be between them. As if he was not so stern, suddenly—so unapproachable. "How novel."

"If you have another preference, you need only make it known." His brows rose a fraction. "I have already notified the local paper. The announcement will be made in tomorrow's edition. Everything else can be expedited."

"Two weeks," she repeated, wishing she could see behind the distant expression he wore like a mask tonight. Her intuition hummed, whispering that something was not as it ought to be, but she dismissed it. *Nerves*, she thought. His as well as hers, perhaps. And well she should be nervous, marrying such a man. He would bulldoze right over her, if she showed the slightest weakness. He might do it anyway. He was doing it now.

And yet some primitive part of her thrilled to the challenge of it. To the challenge of *him*. Even this somber version of him. What did that say about her?

"Two weeks," he said, as if confirming a deal. He settled back against his chair, and picked up his ever-present mobile. "Perhaps you should take the helicopter into Athens and find yourself something to wear."

"Perhaps I will," she agreed, and picked up another crumbled-off piece of the feta, letting the sharp bite of it explode on her tongue. No matter how spicy, or sharp, she always went back for more. She could not fail to make the obvious connection. Perhaps, she thought with some mixture of despair and humor, that was simply who she was.

She did not notice, until much later, that he had not told her *why* he wanted to marry so quickly. That he had talked around it entirely.

Everything seemed to speed up then, making Tristanne feel almost dizzy. Soon they would be married, she told herself, and they would have the rest of their lives to sort through whatever lay beneath his sudden remoteness. She told herself that this was simply the male version of jitters—and at least her focus on what Nikos was or was not feeling, or how he was behaving, allowed her to avoid focusing on the things *she* did not want to think about.

He was busy all the time, he claimed. He was always on his mobile, talking fiercely in Greek. When he found time to speak to her, it was to confirm that she was tending to the wedding details he had given over to her. She found a simple dress in a boutique in Athens, as directed. She met with a woman in the capitol city of Argostoli on the island who bubbled over with joy at finding the perfect flowers for Nikos's bride.

She contacted her family. Vivienne, predictably, was overjoyed—her enthusiasm not quite hiding the tremor in her voice, though she tried.

"That is how it was for your father and me," she said with

a happy sigh. "We took one look at each other and everything else was inevitable."

Tristanne could not reconcile the cold parent Gustave had been with the stories her mother told of him, but she did not argue. Once her mother arrived, she would be safe. And soon, Tristanne had no doubt, well. It was all as she'd planned, back when she'd believed she could manipulate Nikos to her will.

"You must come to Greece," she said softly. "We cannot marry without you."

Peter, of course, was more difficult, even after she had the pleasure of telling him she no longer required his help in any respect—that he could keep her trust fund for the next three years, with her compliments.

"You've upped the ante, haven't you?" He sneered into the phone. "How proud you must be of yourself. I had no idea you could make a man like Katrakis turn his thoughts to matrimony. What a perfect little actress you are!"

"You are, in point of fact, my only sibling," Tristanne said coldly. "That is the only reason I am extending an invitation."

"That and the fact it would look powerfully odd if I did not attend," Peter shot back. "Never fear, Tristanne. I will be there."

She rather thought that sounded like a threat.

But there was no time to worry about Peter and whatever new atrocity he might be planning. Tristanne was infinitely more concerned about her husband-to-be, whose demeanor seemed to grow colder and more unapproachable by the hour as the clock ticked down to their wedding day.

If it were not for the nights, she would have panicked. But he came to her in the darkness, without fail. She would lie awake until his dark form appeared, crawling over her on the wide bed. Silent and commanding, he made love to her with a fierce urgency that she felt sear her all the way to her soul.

He held her in the aftermath, close to his chest, his hands tangled in her hair, and he never said a word.

She should talk to him, she reasoned in the light of day. She should interrupt one of his interminable business calls and ask him what was bothering him. She would have, she told herself, were she not able to perfectly envision the kind of mocking set-down he might deliver. He was not the kind of man who could be asked about his feelings. She was not even certain if he was aware that he had any.

The truth was, she missed him. She missed his teasing, their sparring—that half smile of his and the gleam of old coin gold in his dark eyes—but the sudden stiffness between them felt precarious, like something fragile stretched across a great morass of darkness. Tristanne was afraid to poke at it.

That was the real reason, of course, she admitted to herself only when she was standing alone with the Greek sunlight drenching her in its shine. She was terrified that if she mentioned anything—anything at all—he would think better about all the ways she had deceived him and change his mind. And she could not bear to think of losing him.

It was as simple—as wretchedly, starkly simple—as that.

She could not imagine a day without his touch, without looking at that hard, beautiful face. Without seeing those deep gold eyes, those haughty cheekbones. Without feeling the heat of that steely chest. She did not want to imagine it.

She knew that she should loathe herself for falling so hard, so heedlessly—for risking so much. For being, as Peter had always told her, so very like her poor mother. But try as she might, she could not seem to gain the necessary distance. It was as she'd sensed it would be from the start. Perhaps as she'd imagined when he'd left her breathless at that ball so long ago. The moment she'd let her defenses down, and let him in, she had been forever altered. She wanted him more, it seemed, than she wanted to keep herself safe.

She could only hope she would not have to choose between the two.

It was like déjà vu.

Nikos stood on the deck of his yacht and watched the well-dressed and well-preserved guests mingle with each other in front of him. He, too, was dressed exquisitely in a beautifully tailored Italian suit, as befitted the host and the bridegroom on the night before his wedding was supposed to take place. But he could not seem to pay the proper amount of attention to his business associates or the expected luminaries who milled about, drinking his wine and laughing too loudly into the coming evening. He could not even pay his respects to the coast of his beloved Kefallonia as the boat slowly moved past this stunning cliff, that hidden gem of a beach and yet another picturesque village. It was all a blur to him.

He only had eyes for Tristanne.

She wore something blue tonight that seemed spun from clouds, so effortlessly did it dance over her curves, calling attention to the bright spark in her warm eyes, the golden glow of her skin. Her hair swept over her shoulders in dark blonde waves, calling to mind the golden Kefallonian sands as they basked beneath the Greek sky. She was too alive, too vibrant. Too beautiful.

And he was keenly aware that this was the last night she would seem so. That he would crush the very thing he found so intoxicating about her from her as surely as if he planned to do it with his own foot.

He could not make sense of the churning in his gut, or his own inability to carry through with his plan with all the comfort of the righteousness that had been his only companion these many years. Why should he regret that she must feel the consequences of her family's actions? That she must pay for the loss of three lives? Why should he regret anything?

As if she could feel his gaze upon her, she turned away from the guests she was talking to and smiled at him. He watched her excuse herself with a word and her perfect social smile, and then he allowed himself to sink into the vision of her as she crossed the deck to him.

He let himself pretend, for just one moment, that she would truly become his bride in the morning. *His wife.*

He could not deny the sense of rightness that spread through him then, spiraling out from the part of him that had told him she was his since the start and taking him over in a heady kind of rush. But it did not matter what he *felt*, he reminded himself grimly, forcing himself back under control. It only mattered what he did. What he had vowed he would see through to the bitter end.

"You look forbidding," she said, her voice light, though her eyes searched his. He caught the faintest hint of her perfume, something fresh and enticing, that made him want to put his mouth on her. He did not know how he refrained.

"I find I am less interested in parties than I was once," he said. He tugged at the collar of his shirt, wishing they were hidden away in the villa, where he would already be naked and she would already be astride him. Why could it all not be as simple, as elemental as that?

She smiled, as if she could read his mind. "This party is in your honor," she pointed out, angling her body toward his. "You could smile. Or at least stop frowning. I don't think it would ruin your mystique."

He smiled without meaning to, and then wondered how he could be so susceptible to her. How he could let his control slip so easily. He had ignored the way she had watched him over the past weeks, her brown eyes grave and thoughtful. He had ignored the way he had gone to her, then held on to her as if he could hold back the night, keep reality at bay. He had ignored everything.

But tonight, his resolve seemed to have been left behind when the boat left the shore in Assos. He looked at her, her face so open and trusting, and wanted more than anything to be the man she thought he was. The man he ought to be.

But that man did not exist—and what possibility there might have been of his becoming that man had been snuffed out by the Barberys ten years ago. Why was that so hard to remember when she was near?

"And that is important to you?" he asked idly. He wished that it was done. He wished that he had finished with this act of revenge already, and that it was behind him. He told himself it was the drawing out that was killing him, the waiting even now, at the eleventh hour. "You feel I should pretend to be friendly and approachable for the benefit of wedding guests who, presumably, already know perfectly well I am neither?"

She laughed, and it hurt him, though he refused to acknowledge it. Her eyes were so warm, so happy as she looked up at him.

"Oh, Nikos," she said, as if she was still laughing, as if the words bubbled up from within her like a mountain spring, fresh and clean and pure. "I do love you."

He felt himself turn to stone.

He knew who he was. He knew what he must do.

And he did not believe in love.

Even hers.

Tristanne felt him freeze solid beneath her hands. Her words hung there between them, taking over the night, seeming to gather significance—seeming to echo back from the cliffs.

"I did not mean to say that!" she whispered, stricken. Appalled at herself and her carelessness.

He looked like a stranger suddenly—so faraway, so

alien—though he had hardly moved a muscle. Panic and dread exploded inside of her, making her feel almost drugged— heavy and close to tears, where seconds before she had felt like air.

"I'm so sorry," she said hurriedly. "I did not know I was going to say it!"

"Did you not?" His voice was so cold. So distant. Condemning. "Perhaps you meant it in the casual way. The way one loves a car. Or a shoe."

He sounded almost uninterested. Almost as if he was poking at her as he'd used to. But Tristanne could see something that looked like anguish in his eyes, turning them very nearly black.

She sucked in a breath, skimmed her hands over his wide shoulders. Took another breath, and met his gaze. For a moment she did not know if she could do this. She, who had stood up to him when her very knees threatened to give out. She, who had argued with him when she would have been better-served trying to protect herself.

But if she could not keep herself safe, she could pretend to be brave.

"I did not mean to say it, but it's true," she said, her voice soft, but sincere. "I do, Nikos. I love you."

He only stared at her, as the party seemed to dim and disappear around them. His eyes were so dark as he looked down at her, with no hint at all of gold. No trace of something like tenderness she'd thought she'd seen there on occasion. It was almost as if he could not make sense of her words.

Something passed between them, heavy and unspoken, thick. Tristanne felt her eyes well up, though she did not cry, and saw a muscle twitch in his jaw—though she sensed he was not angry. He was nothing so simple as *angry*.

"This wedding has addled your brain," he said, hoarsely, after moments—or years—had passed. "How can you love me, Tristanne? You hardly know me. You have no idea what I am capable of!"

She remembered the words she had thrown at him on the cobblestones in Portofino, and shivered involuntarily. Had that been foreboding? A premonition? Had she been waiting, since then, for the other shoe to fall?

"I know you," she said softly. She squared her shoulders, and met his gaze straight on. "Better than you think."

"Very well then," he said then, biting the words out. So cold, so far away suddenly. "I hope that knowledge brings you great comfort in the days to come."

"You mean when we are married?" she asked, not quite following him, but feeling somehow that they were poised on the edge of a great disaster.

"Yes," he said, his mouth twisting, bitterness thick in the air between them, though she could not understand it. "When we are married."

CHAPTER FIFTEEN

TRISTANNE stood before the floor-length mirror in the villa's master suite, staring at the vision before her. Her hair was caught back in a clasp at her crown, then tumbled about her bare shoulders in a cascade of dark blonde waves. The ivory dress clasped her tight around the bodice, then skimmed to the ground, light and airy, simple and elegant. Her makeup was flawless, calling attention to her eyes, her lips, and making her complexion seem to be a deep cream, with a glow within. She wore her mother's pearls and behind her, near to the chair where Vivienne sat clasping her hands to her chest in delight, a bouquet bursting with fragrant white flowers graced a low table.

Tristanne was the perfect vision of the perfect bride. And yet she could not seem to shake the terrible sense of foreboding that had gripped her ever since Nikos had left her side the night before. Ever since she had told him she loved him and he had stared at her as if he'd never laid eyes on her before. She trembled again, now, thinking of it.

"You are a beautiful bride!" Vivienne cried from behind her, as if she were neither fragile nor upsettlingly pale.

"Am I?" Tristanne was hardly aware of having spoken. She felt as if she was in a dream. How could this be her wedding day? How could she be dressed to marry a man that she did not quite trust, who did not love her, who might never care for her as she did for him? How could it all have come to this? Surely, on this day of all days, she should feel some kind of certainty about the man she was about to vow to spend the rest of her life with. Instead all she could see was that odd, cold look in Nikos's dark eyes last night. All she could feel was a low-level panic, making her faintly nauseous, slightly dizzy. And she could not seem to do anything but stare at herself, as if her reflection held the answers, were she only to look hard enough.

The logical part of her mind knew exactly what she should do. It had spent the long night drawing up exit strategies and outlining escape plans. She could not possibly marry a man who had reacted to her declaration of love in such a way. A man whom she did not trust, who, as he had said himself, she barely knew. What was she thinking? She was the result of a hasty marriage, had grown up watching her mother beg for the scraps of her father's attention—and she had vowed she would never put herself in that position. How could she possibly sentence herself to the very same fate?

But the logical part of her mind was not the part that had dressed in this gown, allowed her hair to be teased into place or her makeup to be applied with such care by her attendants. The logical part of her had nothing to do with the serene bridal vision she saw reflected in her mirror. And the truth was that Tristanne had no idea what she should do—what she *wanted* to do.

Except…that was not the truth, was it?

Tristanne felt something click into place inside of her then, as realization finally dawned, the fog that had invaded her brain seeming, finally, to clear.

A woman who was appropriately appalled by the fact that Nikos had, very clearly, wanted nothing to do with her declaration would have done something about it. She might have left, called off the wedding, or found Nikos to demand that he explain himself. A woman who was not afraid to push the issue would…have pushed. But Tristanne was afraid. She was afraid that if pushed, Nikos would disappear. Hadn't she been afraid of this very thing since the evening he had proposed? So instead, she had allowed herself to be carried along by the age-old rituals of the bride's toilette. She had chosen what she wanted by pretending not to choose.

"You must come and see," Vivienne said then, her thin, breathy voice breaking in to Tristanne's reverie. "Look at this fine sight, Tristanne!"

Tristanne blinked, feeling as if she was waking from some kind of drugged sleep. She turned to find that her mother had moved across the room to peer out of one of the windows that looked out over the villa's sculpted gardens where the civil ceremony was supposed to take place. Tristanne walked over to join her there, feeling the caress of her gown against her legs, the brush of her curls against her shoulders. Her skin felt too sensitive, as if Nikos was in front of her, that half smile on his dark face and molten gold in his eyes. Her body knew what it wanted. What it always wanted and, she feared, always would. No matter what.

She stood at her mother's side and looked down into the sun-kissed garden. Guests were already taking their seats in the rows of chairs set to face the gleaming blue sea. White flowers flowed from baskets, and birds sang from above. It was a beautiful scene—as if ripped from the pages of some glossy wedding magazine and brought to life.

All that was missing was the groom.

"No, I am sure he will come," Tristanne said at first, when the appointed time had come and gone. The guests' murmurs had turned to open, speculative conversation that Tristanne could hear all too well from the windows above.

But he did not come. Fifteen minutes became thirty. Then forty-five minutes, then an hour, and still Nikos did not appear.

"He would not do this," Tristanne said, her voice wooden. She had said it several times already—to her mother's drawn and anxious face, to her increasingly furious brother—both before and after the necessary announcement had been made to the assembled guests.

She had shut herself down. Her stomach might heave, her head might spin, and she might be fighting back tears that seemed to come from her very soul—tears she was afraid to give into because she did not think she would ever stop—but she would not show it. *She could not show it!*

"Would he not?" Peter spat this time, whirling to face her. "He has no doubt lived for this moment for the past ten years!"

"You do not know what you're talking about," Tristanne said, automatically jumping to Nikos's defense, even as she heard the desperate edge in her voice. How could this be happening? How could he have done this?

Please…she cried inside her mind. But she remembered that bitter undercurrent to his words. That bleak look in his eyes.

"It had to be Nikos Katrakis, didn't it?" Peter sneered. His pacing had rendered him red-faced and slightly shiny, and his cold eyes slammed into her. Ordinarily she would heed these warning signs and try to maintain a safe distance from Peter's rage—but she could not seem to move from the chair she had sunk into when the clock had struck an hour past the time she had been meant to walk down the aisle. She could only stare at him, willing herself not to break down.

Not in front of Peter. She had never broken down in front of Peter. Not even when he used his hands.

"I don't know what you mean," she said, with admirable calm. From a distance, she thought, she might even look calm, while inside she thought she might already have died.

"You had to pick out the one man alive who could make our situation worse! We will be the laughingstock of Europe!"

Peter hissed. "I knew this would happen—I *told* you this would happen! You selfish, irresponsible—"

"That's rich, coming from you," Tristanne heard herself saying, with fight and spirit that felt completely foreign to her. As if she cared about Peter, or, perhaps, it was that she no longer cared at all, about anything. "I am not the one who lost the family fortune."

She heard her mother gasp in horror, but she could not tend to Vivienne just then. She could not even tend to herself. She could only sit there, her hands clenched in her lap, her dress stiff and uncomfortable all around her, trying to make sense of what was happening. *What could not be happening.* What was, it became clear with every passing second, really and truly happening after all.

He would not do this! something inside of her howled. Not after she had told him everything. Not after all that had passed between them. She thought of that archway in Florence—the way that he had held her then. The fierce, consuming way he had made love to her. So raw, so desperate. How could none of that be real?

Peter laughed, unpleasantly. "I hope you enjoyed your low-class love affair while it lasted, Tristanne. I hope it was worth the humiliation we will now face in front of the entire world! Our father must be turning over in his grave!"

"Something must have happened to him," Tristanne said, but even she could not believe it at this point. Two hours and thirty-six minutes, and Nikos was not here. He was not coming. *He was not coming.* Though, in truth, she was still hoping. That he had been in a car accident, perhaps. His broken body in a hospital bed, and wouldn't they all be so ashamed of their revolting speculation—

But then there was a commotion near the door, and one of his servants stood there, looking embarrassed. And she knew before he said a single word.

"I am so sorry, miss," he said, not making eye contact,

wringing his hands in front of him. "But Mr. Katrakis left this morning. He took the helicopter into Athens, and he has no plans to return."

Tristanne got up then. It was that or simply collapse into herself. She launched herself to her feet, and moved away from the chair, looking desperately around the stark, white room as if something in it might calm her, or make this nightmare better somehow. *He has no plans to return.*

"What a surprise," Peter snapped, advancing on her. His face was screwed up with rage, and that black hatred that had always emanated from him in waves. "He remembered that he is a Katrakis and you are a Barbery! Of course he could not marry you! Of course he chose instead to humiliate you! I should have expected this from the start!"

"I have no idea what you're talking about," she told Peter, through lips that felt numb. She wanted to scream, to run, to hide…but where on earth could she possibly go? Her old life in Vancouver? How could it possibly fit her now? How could she ever pretend she had not felt what she had felt, nor loved as she still loved, even now, in the darkest of moments? It was choking her. Killing her. And she had the strangest feeling that even should she survive the horror of this moment, what she felt would not diminish at all. She knew it in the exact same, bone-deep way that she had known that Nikos Katrakis would ruin her. *She knew it.*

"Did you think he wanted *you*, Tristanne?" Peter hissed. "Did you imagine he was sufficiently enamored of your charms? The only thing you had that Katrakis wanted was your name."

"My name?" She felt as thick, as stupid, as Peter had always told her she was. "Why would he care about my name?"

"Because he loathes us all," Peter threw at her. "He swore he would have his revenge on us ten years ago, and congratulations, Tristanne—you have handed it to him on a silver platter!"

"Peter, please," Vivienne murmured then. "This is not the time!"

But Tristanne was watching her brother's expression, and a prickle of something cold washed over her.

"What did you do?" she asked. Her fists clenched, as if she wanted to protect Nikos from Peter—but no, that could not be what she felt. She wanted to make sense of what was happening, that was all. There had to be a reason he had abandoned her—there had to be! "What did you do to him?"

"Katrakis is nothing but trash," Peter snapped. "Ten years ago he had ideas above his station. He got in over his head in a business deal, and could not handle himself. He lost some money, made some threats." He shrugged. "I was astounded he ever made anything of himself. I expected him to disappear back into the slime from which he came."

"Then let me ask you another way," Tristanne said coldly, Nikos's words spinning through her head, their whole history flashing past her as if on a cinema screen. "What does he think that you did?"

"I believe he blames me for any number of things," Peter said dismissively. "He had a rather emotional sister, I believe, who fancied herself in love and then claimed she was pregnant." He scoffed, and made a face. "He blamed me when she overdosed on sleeping pills, but his own mother was a known drug user. I rather think blood tells, in the end." His lip curled. "Look at yours."

Vivienne made a soft sound, and something ignited inside of Tristanne. She waited to feel the usual wave of shame, of anger, that someone who should love her should find her so disgusting, so worthless. But it never came. All she could think was that this was how her brother chose to speak to her just after she had been left at the altar. This was how he chose to behave. And the worst part was that it was in no way a departure from his usual behavior. He had treated her this way for years—and she had allowed it, because better her than her mother. But why would he stop, now that Gustave was gone? Soon, she had no doubt, he would turn it on her mother directly, and she could not have that.

She had not gone through this, all of this, to watch Peter destroy Vivienne as she knew he wished to do—as he had already tried to do. She did not know how she would survive the next moment, or the next breath, with the vast, impossible pain that ate her from the inside out. She wondered who she was now that it was over, now that Nikos had left her, and how she might ever put the pieces of herself back together. She had no idea what might become of her.

But she was still standing, and maybe that was all that mattered. For as long as she could stand, she could protect her mother. Which was why she was here in the first place.

"You are a monster," she said softly, but distinctly, to Peter. "I do not think there is a shred of humanity within you. Not one shred."

Peter moved closer, his face set into a scowl. Yet Tristanne did not step away. Or shrink back. After all, what could he do to her that Nikos had not already done? Threaten her? Bruise her? Why should she care? The worst had already happened. She was a fool in the eyes of the world, and worse, she was in love with the man who had abandoned her. She had no idea how she would ever get past this. She had no idea where she would start. How could Peter possibly compete?

"You had better watch yourself, *sister*," he hissed, his voice menacing.

It was the word *sister* that rang in her, then. That ricocheted inside of her and made her realize that he had never honored that term, not even when they were children. At least her father, for all that he had been cold and dismissive, had performed his fatherly duties. He had fed her, clothed her, paid for her schooling until he no longer felt he could support her choices. And perhaps Nikos had been right to make her question the appropriateness of those choices. It had hurt her at the time that Gustave could not be more supportive of her—but then, that was not at all who Gustave Barbery had been. He might not have been the best father she could have hoped for, but at least he had been a father.

What had Peter ever done? Tristanne, who had never asked him for anything, had asked him for access to her trust fund a few years early and what was his response? To whore her out at his command, for his purposes. And now, in the worst moment of her life, abandoned at the altar on her wedding day—still wearing her wedding dress—he behaved liked this. If she could have felt something beyond the agony of Nikos's betrayal, she might have felt sick.

"I am not your sister," she told him, feeling more free in that moment than ever before. "I don't know why I ever cared to honor the relationship when you, clearly, do not. Consider it ended."

"How dare you—" he began.

She turned her back on him, and looked wildly around, her gaze landing on her mother. Beautiful, vibrant Vivienne, so diminished now. So delicate. She was the only family Tristanne had ever had. The only thing worth protecting. And she was worth this, Tristanne told herself fiercely. Her mother was worth any price, no matter how heavy.

"Mother," she said, her voice rough enough to be a stranger's. But then, she felt like a stranger to herself, almost as if she inhabited someone else's body. A body Nikos would never love again, never taste again; a body that would never melt into his—she shook the thoughts away, and bit back the sob that threatened to spill out. "I must change out of these clothes, and then we are leaving this place."

"Where will we go?" Vivienne asked, like a child, her voice soft. Weak. It only hardened Tristanne's resolve.

"You will go directly to Salzburg," Peter ground out behind

her. "Or I will cut you both out like the parasites you are. Do you hear me?"

"Do what you must," Tristanne said offhandedly—only to gasp when he reached over and grabbed her arm, hauling her toward him as he had many times before, his fingers digging into the flesh of her arm.

"Where do you think you're going?" he demanded. "Your pathetic life in Canada? You are useless and *she* makes you look industrious! Do you imagine you can *both* work on your backs?"

Tristanne heard Vivienne's shocked exclamation, but she focused on Peter's hard, cold eyes, and let all of her pain and rage build inside of her.

"I doubt my imagination is half so vivid as yours," she spat at him. She jerked her arm out of his grasp, shoving back from him with a force that surprised them both. He was stronger than her—and a true bully—but he did not expect her to push back. He dropped his hand. She moved around him, heading for the dressing room door.

"This is all very impressive, but we both know you'll come crawling back to me within the month," he snarled. "Don't think I will be as generous with you as I was this time."

"Believe me," she threw over her shoulder, her sarcasm practically burning her tongue. "I am well aware of the limits of your generosity."

He laughed at her. "And what exactly do you think will become of you, Tristanne?" he taunted her.

She looked back then. For the last time. She knew in that moment that she would never see Peter again. And in the midst of all the rest of the pain, the horror, that she was not certain she would ever sort out, it ignited one small flare of hope.

"I will survive," she told him, and she knew, somehow, that she would. "No thanks to you."

All she had to do was keep standing.

CHAPTER SIXTEEN

NIKOS sat in his favorite small bar in Athens, drinking the most expensive liquor available, and told himself he was celebrating.

He had been celebrating in this manner for weeks now. He had so much to celebrate, after all. He should be overjoyed. The pictures of his aborted, abandoned wedding were in all the papers, the humiliation for the Barberys as extreme as he'd anticipated. He had it on excellent authority that Peter Barbery's investors had abandoned him, and the Barbery fortunes were in free fall. Peter was expected to declare bankruptcy before the year was out, whether he had faced this truth or not.

At first, Nikos told himself that the odd feeling that claimed him was no more than the usual letdown after a particularly long campaign. One should expect to feel the absence of focus after living with such a specific goal for so long. It was natural—logical, even. And that was all that it was. There could be no other explanation.

So he told himself while he closed other deals, racing through them like a madman. A chain of hotels in the Far East. A thoroughbred race horse considered highly likely to win the Triple Crown. A boutique inn on the French Riviera that catered to a very elite, very private few. All deals that should have made him feel that his position—his global dominance—was cemented. Unassailable and assured. All deals that would have had him truly celebrating not so long ago. With the prettiest women, the most expensive wine, in the most glamorous places he could find.

Instead he found himself on the same bar stool in this same hidden-away bar that he had once worked in, in another lifetime, bussing tables for the actors and actresses who frequented the place. Tonight he swirled a fine whiskey in his glass and stared at nothing, unable to avoid the truth any further.

He had achieved his ultimate revenge—made all of his dreams come true—and he simply did not care. He had stood at his father's grave, laid flowers for Althea and her lost child and he had not felt a thing. *What a pointless exercise*, he had thought, staring down at a stone marker that commemorated the man who had never cared overmuch for him, the girl who had hated him and the baby who had never had a chance. He had become the man his father would be proud of, finally. He knew this was true the moment he realized he simply could not bring himself to care about the family name he had taken all this time to avenge. It was as if he had turned to stone himself.

He motioned the bartender toward his glass, and stared down at the amber liquid. That emptiness had been the first feeling, and he had denied it, but he had never expected what came behind it. He had never imagined that he, Nikos Katrakis, could *hurt*.

Because he knew that was the only word to describe the agony in his chest, the heat of it, the impossible weight of all that he had lost. He was not ill, as he had first assumed. He simply ached. He could not sleep. He was irritable by day and his head was a vivid mess—and she was the only thing he saw. He imagined what she must have done that day, how she must have felt. He imagined how she had received the news, and how soon she had accepted what, he knew, she could not have wanted to believe could be true. How long had it taken? What had she felt? He tortured himself with images of her tears—or, worse, her bravery. Then, even more insidious, he imagined different endings to the same day. What if he had not left her there? What if he had chosen to marry her despite everything? What if he could lay beside her tonight, smelling the sweet scent of her hair, the faint musk of her skin?

What if he had let himself believe her when she'd claimed to love him?

Nikos growled under his breath, cursing himself in every language he knew. Now that he had done what he set out to do, he could not see how it had consumed him for so long. What had he won? What had he achieved? Why did it all feel like so much wasted breath and misery, for absolutely no reason?

How could he have prized a loyalty to people who had disdained him over what he should have owed to Tristanne—the only person in all his life who had looked at him with joy in her eyes, however briefly? She had told him that she loved him, and he had responded by abandoning her at the altar. He was no better than an animal. He was exactly the kind of scum he had spent his life attempting to distance himself from. He, who had always vowed that he would never be Peter Barbery, had become something far worse. At least Peter had ended things with Althea himself—he had not allowed his absence to speak for him.

What kind of man was he, that he could have done what he had done?

"She is not worth it, my friend," the bartender said, shaking Nikos out of his brooding contemplation of his whiskey.

Nikos focused on him, surprised that the man dared to speak to him after weeks of careful silence.

"Is she not?" he asked lightly. "How do you know?"

"She never is," the man said. He shrugged. "What do they

say? You can't live with them and you can't live without them, yes? It is always the same old story."

He moved down the bar to answer another patron's demands, but Nikos felt frozen into place. It was as if a light had gone off inside of him, and he finally, finally understood.

He was not a man who wallowed—nor one who ever backed down from a challenge, even if the challenge was of his own making. He had more money than he could ever spend. He had homes in every city that had ever caught his eye. He had come from nothing, and now he had everything. And none of it meant anything to him without Tristanne. He could not live without her scowl, her defiant chin, her thoughtful brown eyes. He did not *want* to live without her, no matter what her last name was, no matter who her family were, no matter what.

He could not feel this way. It could not continue. He could not live without her. It was as simple as that.

Everything else was negotiable.

Tristanne was not surprised, necessarily, when the sleek black car pulled to a stop beside her as she walked back along the avenue toward the little house she and Vivienne had rented when they'd first arrived back in Vancouver. She was not *surprised* when Nikos unfolded himself from the back of the car, his long, hard frame as lethally graceful as she remembered.

But that did not mean she was happy about it, either—to look up from her life and see him. To feel him steal all the light from the world and the breath from her body. She stopped dead in her tracks, a carrier bag swinging from her arm, and stared.

He had commanded all the light in the sunlit glory of the Mediterranean; on a street in a Vancouver neighborhood, gray with the start of the fall rains, he was magnificent—like a supernova, for all that he was dressed in black. Dark black sweater, charcoal-colored trousers and that sleek black hair that very nearly tousled at the ends. Tristanne ignored the wild tumult of her heart, her nerves, her stomach as he moved toward her. He looked graver than she remembered—more grim. No hint of that half smile on his full lips, no gleam at all in his tea-steeped eyes.

She told herself she was glad. That it made him a stranger to her. And there was no need at all for her to talk to a stranger.

"I imagine you hate me," he said, coming to a stop in front of her.

For a moment she could only blink. Then Tristanne felt a wave of something deep and messy wash over her, through her. Rage? Grief? She could not distinguish between the two.

"No preamble?" she threw at him. "No greeting, even? Do I deserve so little from you, Nikos? Not even the sort of courtesy you would extend to a stranger?"

She started moving then, jerky and rough, but she could not stay there. She could not look at him. She needed to barricade herself in her new bedroom, cry into her pillow and tell herself that she did not still yearn for a man who could treat her like this. *She could not.*

"Did you mean what you said?" he asked. He kept pace with her with no apparent effort, which made her even more furious.

"We said a great many things, you and I," she muttered, scowling at the ground. "One of us meant what was said and the other was nothing but a very practiced liar—so you will have to be more specific."

She could not seem to keep her composure any longer. She had cried more in the past weeks than she had in the previous long years of her life. She hardly recognized herself anymore. She was what he had made her—this smashed, ruined, broken thing.

"You are crying," he said, as if he was horrified. She stopped walking and whirled on him, wishing she was stronger, bigger. Wishing she could make him feel what she felt. Wishing she could hurt him.

"I do that often," she snapped. "Congratulations, Nikos. You undid almost thirty years of self-control in one day."

"And yet this is the man you claimed to love," he said, his voice darker and rougher than she remembered. Almost as if he hurt, too, though she knew that must be impossible. "This monster, who would do this terrible, unforgivable thing!"

"I know what you did," she gritted out. "You did it to me. But why are you here? What could you possibly want?" She laughed then, the kind of laugh that was torn from inside of her, hollow and broken. "I have to tell you, Nikos—I do not think there is anything left."

"I am not a man worth loving," he told her. "You were a fool to say such a thing to me, to admit to such a weakness. You should count yourself lucky that I did not believe you— that I did not hold you to such an insane pledge."

She opened her mouth to scream at him, to demand he leave her before she broke into even tinier fragments, but something stopped her. His eyes were too dark. His mouth was too hard. If he was another man, she would have said he looked almost…desperate.

"Is that why you came all the way to Vancouver?" she asked him, her voice uneven. "To explain to me why I should not have fallen in love with you?"

"There is nothing in me worth loving," he said, his gaze intent. "You need only look at my history. My mother. My father. My sister. All these people abandoned me, hated me. All of them. One family member, perhaps, could be excused away as an anomaly, but all of them? One must look to the common denominator, Tristanne. One must be logical."

"Logical," she managed to say. She shook her head, as if

that could make what he said make sense. "You think this is logical? You truly do, don't you?"

She searched his face, that dark face she had never thought she'd see again, though in the dark of night, when she could no longer hide painful truths from herself, she'd *hoped*. She saw the truth in it—that he believed what he said. That he had not believed her when she'd said she loved him. That he did not—could not—know what love was. It made her ache. For him, in ways she knew she should not.

"It is as if you have some hold on me," he said, his voice almost accusing. "I spent years dreaming of revenge, and now I dream only of you. I destroy everyone I touch." He shook his head. "I am a curse."

Hadn't she said the same thing herself? Hadn't she screamed it into her pillow to muffle the noise, so as not to disturb her mother? So why, now, did she feel herself frowning up at him, as if she wished to contradict him? As if she wanted to argue with him—make him treat himself better than he had ever treated her?

What was the matter with her?

She looked around as if she might find help, or answers, on the sidewalk. But the day was chilly and wet. Everything was gray, except for Nikos, and that hard look in his eyes that made her want to cry and not, for once, for herself.

She could not pretend to herself—when he stood in front of her, when he was within reach, when her palms itched to touch him and her body ached to press against him—that her feelings had changed at all. She wanted it all to have disappeared, or for the anger and betrayal to have bleached away what she'd felt for him.

"I can't blame you for hating me," he said quietly. He shoved his hands into the pockets of his trousers, and she had the distinct impression that he was uncomfortable. He, who had never seemed to show the slightest bit of uneasiness. It sent an arrow spearing through her, piercing through her anger, making it wither away, leaving the maelstrom beneath.

"I want to hate you," she said, with more honesty than he deserved. "But I don't."

"You should," he bit out. "If you had any sense of self-preservation at all, you would."

"You are the expert," she retorted. "Aren't you? Hate, revenge, deceit. I believe that is your forte, not mine. I merely wanted to marry you. More fool, me."

"I do not care about revenge!" he burst out. "I wish I had never heard the word!"

"How can that be true?" she asked, dashing the wetness from her eyes with the backs of her hand. "Peter told me. What he did to you. To your family. To your sister—"

"My sister took her own life, with her own hand. Nothing Peter did can match what I did to you," Nikos said, in that low, painful voice. "I promise you."

"You promise me," she echoed. She laughed again, another hollow sound. "Please, Nikos. Do not make me any more promises. I do not think I can survive them!"

He looked at her for a long moment, those dark eyes seeing into her, through her. Seeing far more than they should.

"I cannot pretend I did not deceive you, because I did. I do not deserve you, Tristanne, but…" His eyes when they met hers were so dark. Tortured. His hands reached out, but did not touch her. "Please believe me," he whispered. "I cannot let you go."

She felt the truth of things well up in her, then, despite everything. She felt that fierce, uncompromising love for him soar through her, making her feel both impossibly dizzy and firmly grounded at the same time. It moved through her like the blood in her veins. Like the air in her lungs. An irrevocable biological necessity without which she could not walk, talk, *live*. And so she knew why she could not run away. Why she could not bring herself to leave him here on the street, as she should. Why she would not abandon him, even when he all but told her to do so.

My dragon, she thought, and it felt like a promise. A vow.

She could not remember who she had been before him, or who she had tried to be during these past weeks. She could not imagine a future without him in it. She had…simply kept standing, because there was nothing else to do. But now that he was here, she could feel the difference singing through her, lighting her up from within, even though it hurt—even though none of this was easy, and all of it was far more painful than she could ever have imagined she could bear.

"Tristanne," he said, as if her name was a plea. His eyes were agonized, as dark and stormy as she felt. "I tried to let you go, but I cannot do it."

She reached over and took his hand, exulting in the feeling of his skin against hers, the heat of him, the sense of *rightness* that flooded through her. What else could she do? She had already lost everything, and survived it. He had already done his worst. And even so, she loved him. She could not hide from that inconvenient truth. It might not be wise. It might not make sense. But the inescapable truth of it felt like heat, like dragonfire, and burned its way through her, marking her forever. As his.

"Then do not let me go," she said over the lump in her throat, looking at him with all she felt bright and hot in her gaze. Because she had already chosen, long ago, to be brave if she could not be safe. She had already decided. "If you dare."

CHAPTER SEVENTEEN

"WHAT am I to do with you?" he asked her much later, his voice rough. He sat next to her in the luxurious depths of his private jet's leather seats. Far below them, North America was spread out like a patchwork quilt, and above them was nothing but blue sky and sun. He reached over and pulled a blonde wave into his hand, wrapping it around one finger. He tugged on it slightly.

"Marry me, apparently," she said. She did not shiver away from his dark golden gaze. She leaned closer. She had wanted him when she was just a girl. She had chosen him on his yacht, so long ago now. Then in the villa. And again, just yesterday, on a street in Vancouver. She had chosen *him*. "That is why we are flying across the world, isn't it?"

"And what makes you think you can handle such a thing?" he asked, searching her face with a deep frown marring his. "I warn you, Tristanne, I do not improve upon a longer acquaintance. Familiarity breeds—"

"Contempt?" she finished for him. She wanted to kiss him, though she did not dare, not when he was in so dark a mood. "Surely not. You are Nikos Katrakis. Who alive could be more fascinating?"

"I am not joking." His voice was stark, and she understood, suddenly, that he was terrified. This strong, harsh, ruthless man. She had this power over him. She reached over and put a hand on his muscled thigh.

You must love who you love, Vivienne had said with a shrug when Tristanne had haltingly explained that, indeed, she planned to marry Nikos after all, despite everything. *And it is only cowards who do not follow their hearts, Tristanne. Remember that.*

"I am not from your world, much as I pretend to be," Nikos said, almost more to himself than to Tristanne. He drummed his fingers against the polished armrest. "People enjoy my money, my power, but do not mistake it—they never forget where I came from."

"Nor should they," she shot back at once. His head snapped around in surprise. "You say that as if it is something shameful. There is no shame in your past, Nikos. You overcame near-insurmountable obstacles, and you did it with absolutely no help from anyone. Not even your own father." She shook her head. "You should be proud."

"You do not understand," he began.

"And who, may I ask, finds it so impossible to overlook your origins?" she asked, cutting him off. "People like my brother? Pampered and spoiled, handed vast fortunes made by others? Why should you care what they think?"

He stared at her then, his gaze hotter and more flinty than she had ever seen it. There was no hint of gold there, only dark like the night. Possessive. Implacable. A deep fire that she knew, low in her bones, was for her alone.

"You cannot take it back," he told her, his voice flat. If she did not know him better, she might have thought him unemotional. "If you marry me, Tristanne, that is the end of it."

"As usual," she said, slipping her arm through his and tilting her head back to look at him, so strong and grim against the bright light all around them, flooding into the cabin, "you have it all wrong. This is only the beginning."

And then, finally, she leaned over and pressed her mouth to his.

He knew the moment she woke.

He turned away from the full moon that shone above the dark sea, and watched as the light skimmed into the room and illuminated her. *His wife.*

He had married her in a private ceremony in the very spot he had abandoned her before; the symmetry healing, somehow. And now she was his, forever.

Nikos could not seem to get his head around the concept.

"What are you doing?" she asked, her voice a mere thread of sound. He moved across the moonlit room to the bed, and lowered himself down to sit beside her. He wanted to take her into his arms again, to lose himself in her body as he had done so many times before—as he had done this very night—but there were too many questions swirling around them and he could not ignore them any longer.

Though part of him wanted to ignore them forever.

"I do not understand," he said quietly.

Next to him, she sat up, pulling the coverlet with her to drape it around her naked shoulders. Her hair tumbled wild and free around her, emphasizing the delicate arch of her collarbone, the creamy softness of her skin. She was exquisite. And she was *his*. She had chosen him, after everything.

"What is there to understand?" she asked, that warm humor lacing her tone, making him nearly forget himself. "It is the middle of the night. Surely understanding can wait until dawn."

"Why would you do this?" he asked, the question ripped from him as if by unseen hands. He did not want to know the answer. Yet he had to know. "After all that I did to you? Why would you not run as fast and as far as you could?"

Her eyes seemed to melt in the darkness, and she reached over to run her fingers along his shoulder, then down to his bicep before dropping her hand back to the bed.

"You already know why."

"Love," he said, harshly. Almost angrily. "Is that what you mean? Love does not exist, Tristanne. It is a lie people tell themselves. A way to hide, to make excuses."

"Here, now, it is real," she said softly, leaning toward him to press her lips against his shoulder. "It is not conditional. You have nothing to prove. It is a fact."

He felt disarmed by that. His heart beat too fast. He felt drunk when he knew he had not touched any spirits in hours. He could not bring himself to look at her, to see whatever lurked in her expression then. Or, perhaps, he was afraid to let her see what was in his own.

"Tomorrow we will leave for our honeymoon," he said instead, his voice too loud in the dark. "The Maldives. Fiji. Whatever you prefer."

"We are already on an island, Nikos," she said in a dry voice, the one that made his heart feel lighter in his chest. "Must we travel great distances to find ourselves on a different one?"

"It is what people do. Or so I am informed."

"Must we worry about what people do?" she asked. "Or shall we worry instead about what we will do?"

He shook his head, unable to answer. Responding to an urge he could not make any sense of, yet could not deny, he slid from the bed and found himself on his knees before her. He ran his palms along her warm thighs, and then gazed up at her. She was heat, warmth. She had melted away all of his defenses.

"I love you," she said. Her tough chin tilted into the air, daring him to argue with her. Daring him not to love her, just as she had dared him not to leave her. She was the bravest woman he had ever known.

"I do not know what love is," he said, the words coming to him as if in a new language. He picked through them carefully. "No one has ever loved me, I do not think. All those who should have—whose obligation it might have been—abandoned me. Hated me."

"I know," she whispered. Her full mouth trembled—for him. She reached for him, ran her fingers through his hair.

"You are the only person who has ever known the truth about me," he managed to say, from that darkness inside of him that he had denied for so long, and that new, strange wellspring of hope that had appeared with her on a Canadian street, so shining and bright and impossible. "The only one who has seen the worst of me, and stayed with me anyway."

She made a soft noise of distress, and then leaned forward to press a kiss against his brow, his cheek.

"I love you," she said simply. "Your darkness as well as your light. How could I do anything but marry you?"

"I told you that you should hate me," he said. "I meant it."

"But it is too late," she whispered. "I have been in love with you since I met you. Perhaps even before. I am the incapable of hating you, I think, despite your best efforts."

"Tristanne…" But he did not know what he could say, except the prayer of hope that was her name. It was like a song in him. He felt that cracking inside of him again, as if he had been buried deep in ice but the long, bitter winter in him had finally ended. And he was starting, at last, to thaw.

"I do not know what love is, or how to go about it," he whispered, looking into the chocolate-colored eyes that were all the world to him now. All that mattered. "But I will spend my life trying to love you as you deserve, Tristanne. I swear it.

Even if you have to teach me, even if it is remedial, I promise I will learn."

She smiled then, a real smile, bright and true. He felt something in him ease, even as he began to burn for her anew. Again. Always.

"I think I can meet that challenge," she said, that strong, sure love in her gaze, changing him as she looked at him. "But first things first, Nikos."

He remembered his own words, long ago, and found himself smiling.

"First things first?" he echoed.

"Why don't you greet me properly?" she dared him. "I am your wife."

"Indeed you are," he said in a low voice. "And I am your husband."

"And this is the first night of our married life. Of the future."

"Our future," he said, and part of him dared to believe in it.

She opened her arms wide, offering him everything he'd ever wanted, and long since ceased hoping for, until she burned her way into his life. Home. Family. Love.

For her, he would dare. For her.

"Then come here," she whispered, her eyes full. "We have a lot of ground to cover."

Harlequin Presents

Coming Next Month

from **Harlequin Presents® EXTRA.** Available March 8, 2011.

Coming Next Month

from **Harlequin Presents®.** Available March 29, 2011.

REQUEST YOUR FREE BOOKS!

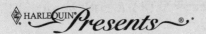

2 FREE NOVELS PLUS
2 FREE GIFTS!

YES! Please send me 2 FREE Harlequin Presents® novels and my 2 FREE gifts (gifts are worth about $10). After receiving them, if I don't wish to receive any more books, I can return the shipping statement marked "cancel." If I don't cancel, I will receive 6 brand-new novels every month and be billed just $4.05 per book in the U.S. or $4.74 per book in Canada. That's a saving of at least 15% off the cover price! It's quite a bargain! Shipping and handling is just 50¢ per book.* I understand that accepting the 2 free books and gifts places me under no obligation to buy anything. I can always return a shipment and cancel at any time. Even if I never buy another book, the two free books and gifts are mine to keep forever.

106/306 HDN E5M4

Name _____ (PLEASE PRINT) _____

Address _____ Apt. #

City _____ State/Prov. _____ Zip/Postal Code

Signature (if under 18, a parent or guardian must sign)

Mail to the **Harlequin Reader Service:**
IN U.S.A.: P.O. Box 1867, Buffalo, NY 14240-1867
IN CANADA: P.O. Box 609, Fort Erie, Ontario L2A 5X3

Not valid for current subscribers to Harlequin Presents books.

Are you a current subscriber to Harlequin Presents books and want to receive the larger-print edition? Call 1-800-873-8635 today!

* Terms and prices subject to change without notice. Prices do not include applicable taxes. N.Y. residents add applicable sales tax. Canadian residents will be charged applicable provincial taxes and GST. Offer not valid in Quebec. This offer is limited to one order per household. All orders subject to approval. Credit or debit balances in a customer's account(s) may be offset by any other outstanding balance owed by or to the customer. Please allow 4 to 6 weeks for delivery. Offer available while quantities last.

Your Privacy: Harlequin Books is committed to protecting your privacy. Our Privacy Policy is available online at www.eHarlequin.com or upon request from the Reader Service. From time to time we make our lists of customers available to reputable third parties who may have a product or service of interest to you. If you would prefer we not share your name and address, please check here. ☐

Help us get it right—We strive for accurate, respectful and relevant communications. To clarify or modify your communication preferences, visit us at www.ReaderService.com/consumerchoice.

HP10R

*Selene wanted nothing to do with the father of her son,
Alex; but Aristedes had other plans...that included them.*

*Read on for an sneak peek from
THE SARANTOS SECRET BABY by Olivia Gates,
available April 2011, only from Harlequin Desire.*

"You were right to turn my marriage offer down," Aristedes said.

And Selene found her voice at last, found the words that
would not betray the blow he'd dealt her. "Thanks for letting me know. You didn't have to come all the way here,
though. You could have just let it go. I left yesterday with
the understanding that this case is closed."

Before the hot needles behind her eyes could dissolve
into an unforgivable display of stupidity and weakness, she
began to close the door.

The door stopped against an immovable object. His flat palm.

"I can't accept that." His voice was low, leashed.

What did her tormentor mean now? Was he ending one
game only to start another?

She raised eyes as bruised as her self-respect to his,
found nothing there but solemnity and determination.

Before she could voice her confusion, he elaborated. "I
never let anything go unless I'm certain it's unworkable. I
realize I made you an unworkable offer, and that's why I'm
withdrawing it. I'm here to offer something else. A work-
ability study."

She leaned against the door, thankful for its support and
partial shield. "Your son and I are not a business venture
you can test for feasibility."

His gaze grew deeper, made her feel as if he was trying
to delve into her mind, take control of it. "It's actually the

other way around. I'm the one who would be tested."

She shook her head. "Why bother? I know—and *you* know—you're not workable. Not with me."

His spectacular eyebrows lowered over eyes she felt were emitting silver hypnosis. "You're right again. Neither you nor I have any reason to believe that isn't the truth. The only truth. It might be best for both you and Alex to never hear from me again, to forget I exist. But then again, maybe not. I'm only asking for the chance for both of us to find out for certain. You believe I'm unworkable in any personal relationship. I've lived my life based on that belief about myself. I never really had reason to question it. But I have one now. In fact, I have two."

Find out what happens in
THE SARANTOS SECRET BABY by Olivia Gates,
available April 2011, only from Harlequin Desire.

MARGARET WAY

In the Australian Billionaire's Arms

Handsome billionaire David Wainwright isn't about to let
his favorite uncle be taken for all he's worth by mysterious
and undeniably attractive florist Sonya Erickson.

But David soon discovers that Sonya's no greedy
gold digger. And as sparks sizzle between them, will
the rugged Australian embrace the secrets of her past
so they can have a chance at a future together?

Don't miss this incredible new tale,
available in April 2011
wherever books are sold!

Harlequin

nocturne™

*Dark and sinfully delicious, Michelle Hauf's
Of Angels of Demons series continues to explore
the passionate world of angels and demons....*

FALLEN

BY MICHELLE HAUF

Fallen Angel Cooper has a steep price to pay, now that he walks the
earth among humans. Wherever the Fallen walk, a demon is not far
behind, intent upon slaying the Fallen in order to claim their own soul.
However, this particular demon strays from her mission, becoming
enamored with the mysterious Fallen Angel. Destined to remain bitter
enemies, the two find themselves entangled in a risky relationship—
with those who want to destroy them hot on their trail.

**"Hauf delivers excitement, danger and romance in a way only she can!"
—#1 *New York Times* bestselling author Sherrilyn Kenyon**

Available in April 2011, wherever books are sold.

Look for the next installment in the
Of Angels and Demons miniseries August 2011.

Harlequin®

A *Romance* FOR EVERY MOOD™

www.eHarlequin.com
www.paranormalromanceblog.com

HNMH61856

HARLEQUIN® HISTORICAL:
Where love is timeless

USA TODAY
BESTSELLING AUTHOR

MARGARET MOORE
INTRODUCES
Highland Heiress

SUED FOR BREACH OF PROMISE!

No sooner does Lady Moira MacMurdaugh breathe a sigh
of relief for avoiding a disastrous marriage to Dunbrachie's
answer to Casanova than she is served with a lawsuit! By
the very man who saved her from a vicious dog attack, no
less: solicitor Gordon McHeath. Torn between loyalty for a
friend and this beautiful woman who stirs him to ridiculous
distraction, Gordon knows he can't have it both ways....

But when sinister forces threaten to upend Lady Moira's world,
Gordon simply can't stand idly by and watch her fall!

**Available from Harlequin Historical
April 2011**

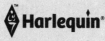

A *Romance* FOR EVERY MOOD™

www.eHarlequin.com

HH29638

Harlequin Blaze

red-hot reads

Sunny, sensual Hawaiian spring break…again!

Three best girlfriends are recapturing an amazing spring-break vacation they had a decade ago.

First on the beach is former attorney and all-around good girl Mia Butterfield. Meeting up with her boyfriend of old is a bust, so she's shocked when her hero turns out to be someone she'd never have expected…

Find out who it is in

SECOND TIME LUCKY

by acclaimed author

Debbi Rawlins

Available from Harlequin Blaze® April 2011

Part of the sensual miniseries,

Spring Break

Part 2: Delicious Do-Over (May)

Harlequin®

A *Romance* FOR EVERY MOOD™

www.eHarlequin.com

HB79607